THE GREAT INDIAN HEISTS

Other books by the Author

True Crime

- The Highway Murders
- Death Served Cold

Crime Fiction

- The Web of Lies
- The Trail of Blood
- In the Shadows of Death
- The Sinners

Short stories
(E-books and Audiobooks)

- The Gift
- The Cookery Show and a Love Story
- A Special Day
- Masks
- An Autumn Turmoil
- The Hunt
- The Death Wish
- Love Beyond 22 Yards
- Crime Beyond 22 Yards
- Loves Lost

THE GREAT INDIAN HEISTS

True Stories of India's Most Dramatic Thefts

SOURABH MUKHERJEE

An imprint of
Srishti Publishers & Distributors

Srishti Publishers & Distributors
A unit of AJR Publishing LLP
212A, Peacock Lane
Shahpur Jat, New Delhi – 110 049

editorial@srishtipublishers.com

First published by Bold,
an imprint of Srishti Publishers & Distributors in 2025

10 9 8 7 6 5 4 3 2 1

This is a work of non-fiction, based on the author's thorough research. Some events have been fictionalised for dramatic effect. While due care has been taken to verify all information at press time, any inadvertent miss brought to notice shall be updated in the subsequent editions.

Printed and bound in India.

Appreciation for the Author and his works

"Sourabh Mukherjee has emerged as one of the front-runners in Indian crime fiction over the last five years."

–Mid-day

"Mukherjee has left his mark on the genre."

–Deccan Herald

"One of the most popular writers of Indian crime fiction."

– The Asian Age

"Death Served Cold is a compelling read based on true events."

– The Times of India

"In Death Served Cold, the author explores the dark recesses of the female psyche."

– IANS

"Death Served Cold reveals shocking excesses of sadism and aggression rarely associated with women."

– Lokmat Time

"The Sinners is a thrilling work of fiction that weaves together elements of corporate warfare and personal vendetta."

– Yahoo News

"The Sinners is definitely the must–read thriller book of the year."

– The Week

"The Sinners is a gripping and riveting read."

– Outlook

"Set in the city of Kolkata, In the Shadows of Death is a fast-paced potboiler which hooks you and keeps you glued to the plot from the very beginning."

– *The Times of India*

"With an almost Freudian understanding of how our childhood experiences influence our adult decisions, Sourabh's novel (In the Shadows of Death) paints a stark picture of urban life in India."

– *The Hindu*

"The theatrical finale comes as much from the extraordinary storytelling as it does from the reveal of the murderer. Mukherjee has the unerring eye of a master craftsman."

– *The Hindu*

"Just when you think you've got it all figured out as per the clues that the killer leaves like crumbs, the author throws you off the path repeatedly with the twists."

–*The News Now*

"A whodunit with several twists, In the Shadows of Death has elements of romance, corporate scandals, and suspense with a strong emotional undercurrent."

– *The New Indian Express*

"A heady concoction of thrill, mystery, psychology and humanity is what makes this book (In the Shadows of Death) such an engrossing fare."

– *Punjab Tribune*

"In the Shadows of Death is crisp, well-composed and there are no loose ends to irk your mind."

– *Yahoo News*

"In the Shadows of Death is a page turner till the end with its fluid narrative infused with twists and revelations, which constantly raise your curiosity level."

– *Zee News*

"A psychological thriller in the true sense of the phrase, In the Shadows of Death delves deep into the psyche of its characters."

– *The Free Press Journal*

"The character of detective Agni Mitra has been rendered in a very believable and realistic fashion. The author has rummaged into the human psyche and used it as the basis for the detective's theories."

– *Tahlka News*

"The novel (In the Shadows of Death) explores the city of Kolkata in a way few contemporary novels have attempted. The City of Joy is not just a backdrop but another character in the novel."

– *Go–Getter, Go Air in-flight magazine*

To the masterminds of heists.

You prove that genius and poor life choices often go hand in hand.

Contents

The Jewel Thief

Harish turned the page of the day's edition of *The Times of India*. He took a sip of the steaming hot tea and started going through the advertisements for open positions. This was now part of his daily routine. Almost a year had passed since his graduation, but all he had managed to find so far were odd jobs with long hours and ridiculously low salaries. His father had retired a few months ago. It was high time Harish took over the responsibility of the family with a stable job and a salary that justified the money his father had spent on his education. Then there was also the question of meeting Arti's father to ask for her hand in marriage. They had been dating for over three years. Arti's family had already started looking for a prospective groom for her, and Harish had to make his move without further delay.

As he scanned the page, his eyes were drawn to an advertisement printed in uppercase letters. It read:

> **WANTED: 50 DYNAMIC GRADUATES FOR THE POSTS OF INTELLIGENCE OFFICER AND SECURITY OFFICER. WALK IN FOR AN INTERVIEW WITH BIO-DATA, CERTIFICATES, AND A PASSPORT-SIZE PHOTO ON 18.03.87 AT THE TAJ INTERCONTINENTAL HOTEL ENQUIRY COUNTER BETWEEN 10 AM AND 5 PM.**

Harish promptly picked up his pen and drew a circle around the advertisement. He was determined not to miss the opportunity. A position in the intelligence department of the government was nothing short of a dream job. With a glint in his eyes and his heart racing, he double-checked the list of documents he was supposed to carry with him for the interview. He was all set. This was the one chance he had been waiting for.

***

Harish pulled out his handkerchief. As he wiped the sweat off his face, his eyes swept across the other candidates who had turned up for the interview.

He had made sure that he arrived at the hotel well before ten in the morning, dressed in his best attire—the white full-sleeved shirt his *Aai* had gifted him after his graduation and had fondly pressed the night before and the black trousers that he wore only on special occasions such as this. The black shoes made from cheap leather had also been treated with a lick of shoeshine. At the enquiry counter in the hotel, he had been informed that the interview was to be conducted in an office at Mittal Towers in Nariman Point. He had lost no time in arriving at the venue, which was not very far from the hotel.

The long queue of candidates who had turned up at the venue was slightly intimidating, but Harish was confident. His gut told him that he would make it. This job meant the world to him.

Harish came out of his reverie when he heard his name being called out. He closed his eyes for a split second and silently offered a prayer, as the faces of his parents flashed before his eyes. He then stood up, checked the contents of the folder he was carrying one last time, straightened his shirt and headed towards the room where the interviews were being conducted.

***

The sun had set, and darkness was slowly descending over the bustling city.

The interview, Harish thought, had gone quite well. The officer who was conducting the interviews had introduced himself as Mohan Singh. He was tall and well-built, with a moustache and hair neatly combed with a parting on the side. He had sharp eyes and spoke in a deep voice that exuded confidence and commanded respect. He was just the kind of man one would expect to be in a position of authority in the Central Bureau of Investigation (CBI).

After the interview, Mohan Singh instructed Harish to wait outside for the final decision. Harish grabbed a quick lunch and quickly returned to the venue.

By the time all the interviews were over, Harish had figured out that at least a hundred and fifty candidates had turned up. What was heartening to observe was that not everyone had been asked to wait for the final results, which meant that Harish had definitely cleared the first round and was in consideration. The question that was now uppermost in Harish's mind was how many out of those shortlisted candidates would eventually be offered jobs in the CBI.

About half an hour had passed since the last candidate had left the room, and Harish's tension was mounting by the minute. When Mohan Singh finally came out of the room with a paper in his hand, Harish's heart leapt into his throat. The advertisement had mentioned that they were looking to hire fifty 'dynamic graduates', and Harish had counted around thirty candidates who had been asked to wait for the final announcement. He had also learnt by conversing with the candidates that some of them already had government jobs but had turned up for the interview, hoping for better opportunities.

'I must thank all of you for taking the time to appear for the interviews today and spending almost the entire day here,' Mohan Singh said, looking at his watch. 'All of you have performed well in the interviews, but after careful consideration, I have selected twenty-six of you for positions in the CBI. I request the others not to lose heart. All of you are smart and knowledgeable, and I convey my best wishes for your bright future. I am sure there are excellent opportunities in store for you. I will now read out the names of the candidates who have been selected for posts in the CBI.'

As Mohan Singh began to read out the names, Harish's heart began to beat so fast that he feared the others in the room would hear it. By the time Mohan Singh had read out fifteen names, Harish's heartbeat had slowed down. When the twentieth name was read out, the first hint of doubt began to raise its ugly head. Harish gave up hope almost completely when the twenty-fourth name was announced. There was a bitter taste in his mouth, and an overwhelming feeling of despair was engulfing him.

The twenty-fifth name was announced.

'Harish Ashtekar, selected for the position of Intelligence Officer in the CBI.' Mohan Singh's voice seemed to reverberate in the room.

For a few seconds, Harish felt numb. Then came the pats on the back from a couple of candidates around him, and his tears broke free.

He had finally made it!

After the last name had been announced and those who had not been selected had departed, Mohan Singh said, 'I request all selected candidates to report to my chamber for further discussion about our next course of action.'

After a few minutes, the twenty-six new recruits of the CBI assembled in the room where Mohan Singh had been conducting the interviews.

'Congratulations and welcome to the CBI,' Mohan Singh said with a smile, which he seemed to have forced with a lot of difficulty. It vanished almost instantly to be replaced by the same serious expression with which he had been conducting interviews through the day.

He continued, 'Gentlemen, as Intelligence Officers and Security Officers working for the country's premier investigative agency, you need to be aware of our motto—Industry, Impartiality, and Integrity. These principles must always guide your work. Loyalty to duty must come first, everywhere, at all times, and under all circumstances. It is our job to uphold the Constitution and the law of the land through honest, impartial, and in-depth investigations. Am I clear?'

'Yes, Sir!' the new recruits replied enthusiastically. Mohan Singh's passionate little speech made them aware of their great responsibility towards the country that had been bestowed on their shoulders in a matter of hours.

'I want all of you to assemble at the Taj Continental at 11 am tomorrow for further instructions. You can leave now. Get a good night's rest as tomorrow will be a busy day,' said Mohan Singh.

Harish stepped out of Mittal Towers with his head held high, his chest thrust forward, and patriotic fervour coursing through his veins. He was now a soldier of his beloved motherland.

***

The vicinity of the Taj Intercontinental Hotel (now, The Taj Mahal Palace) was bustling with the morning crowd. The area offered a unique blend of the rich colonial history and the modern vibrant lifestyle of the city. The hotel itself was a landmark, known for its majestic grandeur. It faced the Arabian Sea and offered stunning views of the Gateway of India, another iconic landmark. The area was also a prime tourist attraction. Visitors from different parts of the country, as well as from faraway lands, had already started pouring in for sightseeing and boat rides as street vendors, photographers, and souvenir sellers crowded around them. BEST buses, cars, and taxis—black-and-yellow, mostly Premier Padmini—crawled lazily along Marine Drive, the popular promenade for locals and tourists alike.

When Harish arrived at the Taj Intercontinental at eleven in the morning the next day, a crowd had already gathered around a big bus that was waiting on the road in front of the hotel. Harish recognised the men standing near the bus. They had all been offered jobs in the CBI the day before. Mohan Singh waited patiently for all the new recruits to turn up, carrying a paper with the list of names, ticking a name off every time a recruit arrived and reported to him. When all twenty-six recruits had assembled in front of the hotel, Mohan Singh instructed them to board the bus.

Once all the recruits had taken their seats inside the bus, Mohan Singh closed the door. He stood facing all the new hires and said, 'Good morning, gentlemen! This is your first day on the job, and I hope all of you are excited and energised.'

Everyone nodded their heads in affirmation.

Mohan Singh continued to speak. 'We have decided to start your onboarding by taking you along on a real mission. All of you will join me in a raid that we will be conducting shortly. As you will agree, there cannot be a better way to learn. You will gain first-hand experience as you watch me in action and I guide you through the process. I am sure today's experience will go a long way in preparing you for the raids and investigations that you will be required to carry out in days to come.'

Mohan Singh paused in case any of the recruits had a question. No one spoke. This was a dream come true for the new recruits.

Mohan Singh then went on, 'But first, I will distribute your CBI identity cards. You are required to display your identity cards when you conduct raids.' He held up a card from a bunch he had in his hand and said, 'Each one of you has earned this. It is something that you will be proud of for the rest of your lives. A big hand to each one of you!'

Everyone clapped enthusiastically.

Mohan Singh then went around the bus, distributing the cards.

When his identity card was handed to him, Harish accepted it gratefully. He looked at the card bearing his photograph and his name, along with the Ashoka insignia. His chest filled with pride. Destiny had kept him waiting, only to offer him an opportunity to be of service to the nation.

Having distributed all the identity cards, Mohan Singh went to the driver and gave him instructions. The bus started shortly.

Mohan Singh returned to his position, facing the recruits and said, 'Our first stop today is the Opera House branch of Tribhovandas Bhimji Zaveri & Sons Jewellers. This jewellery store is among many in the city, about which we have been receiving reports regarding serious discrepancies in terms of weight and the quality of gold being sold. We will be conducting raids in these shops across Mumbai over the next few days.'

As the bus picked up speed, the recruits had mixed feelings. Till that day, they had only read about raids or seen such raids in movies. To be part of a CBI team conducting a raid in a prestigious jewellery store like Tribhovandas Bhimji Zaveri and, that too, on the very first day on the job without any formal training, was both exciting and intimidating. But that was how one learnt on the job! They had complete trust in Mohan*ji*. He had assured them that there was nothing to fear as long as he was around to show them the way.

The bus stopped in front of the Tribhovandas Bhimji Zaveri showroom around a quarter past two in the afternoon.

The Opera House area encapsulated the essence of South Bombay—an eclectic mix of old-world charm, bustling commercial activities, and throbbing community life. The Royal Opera House, though no longer functioning as a theatre, still attracted tourists. The area was the hub of the jewellery business in South Bombay. There were several jewellery shops, big and small, and it was the go-to destination in the city for anyone looking to buy gold, diamonds, or other precious items. The narrow streets bustled with customers, artisans, and small traders. Apart from jewellery, shops dealing in textiles, electronics, and imported goods thrived here. Shops selling daily essentials, newspapers, and snacks lined the pavements. The influence of the Gujarati and Marwari communities, who were heavily involved in the jewellery business, was evident in the cuisine and cultural vibes of the area. The Tribhovandas Bhimji Zaveri showroom stood as a prestigious establishment, drawing affluent clientele.

Mohan Singh opened the driver's chamber, and the officers could see a few briefcases stacked there. He asked the men to pick up the empty briefcases as they alighted from the bus.

'Showtime, gentlemen! Follow me!' Mohan Singh said. Carrying a bag on his shoulder, he sprinted out of the bus.

***

Mohan Singh led the pack as he marched toward the Tribhovandas Bhimji Zaveri showroom in long strides. The officers trooped out of the bus and followed him. The security guards in front of the showroom were momentarily taken aback at the suddenness of the developments and by the size of the army approaching the store. When they regained control of their senses, one of them blocked Mohan Singh's way and opened his mouth to question him about the purpose of his visit with a battalion of men behind him.

Mohan Singh did not let the guard speak. He flashed his card and said, 'We are from the CBI, and this is a raid. Please hand over your guns to my colleagues.' He gestured at two of the recruits to collect the guns from the guards. The security guards complied without questioning.

Once inside the store, Mohan Singh spoke at the top of his voice, announcing that they were from the CBI, and it was a raid. He turned to the recruits following him and asked them to spread out, pointing at different parts of the store with his finger. He approached one of the salespersons and asked for the owner.

The customers in the store looked petrified. Some of them were too shocked to move, and some others headed for the door and were promptly stopped by Mohan Singh and his officers. 'Please do not try to leave the store while the raid is on,' Singh informed the customers politely. 'I request all of you to cooperate with the CBI.'

Before long, Pratap Zaveri, the owner of the store, appeared before Mohan Singh. He was accompanied by a few senior members of his staff. Mohan Singh looked him in the eyes and asked, 'Are you the owner of this store?'

'I am, Sir,' Pratap Zaveri replied, his hands shaking.

'We are from the CBI.' As Mohan Singh spoke, he reached into his pocket and took out a sheet of paper, which he then handed over to Pratap. It was a search warrant. 'We are looking into reports of poor quality of gold in the jewellery being sold in your shop. I would request you and your staff to cooperate with us,' Mohan Singh said, without taking his eyes off Prakash Zaveri for a second.

'There must have been a mistake ...' Prakash tried to speak in self-defence but was interrupted before he could finish.

'Please let the CBI figure that out,' Mohan Singh said in his deep baritone. 'Now, do I have your cooperation in this matter?'

'Of course,' said Zaveri.

Mohan Singh looked around and said, 'I want all CCTV cameras to be turned off.'

Zaveri gestured at one of the staff members who was on his way immediately.

'No one will use the telephone,' said Singh. He turned towards Zaveri and asked, 'Is there a weapon on the premises?'

Zaveri hesitated for a moment.

Singh asked him again, 'I repeat, is there a weapon on the premises?'

'We have a licensed revolver, Sir,' Zaveri declared. 'It's for our protection.'

'Hand it over, please,' Singh said, again gesturing at one of the officers to take possession of the revolver. A member of the staff handed over the revolver to the designated officer shortly.

By this time, the man who had been sent to turn off the CCTV cameras had returned and confirmed having done the same.

Singh turned towards one of his recruits and said, 'Go outside and put up a sign stating that a raid is going on inside the store. Ask the guards to come inside and pull the shutters down.'

'Do you *have* to mention that a raid is going on?' Zaveri tried to protest meekly. 'We have goodwill ...'

Singh again stopped him and said, 'You should have thought about your goodwill before deciding to take your customers for a ride.'

Zaveri threw his hands up in the air in despair. He realised that there was no point in trying to appeal to the CBI officer.

Once the guards had been summoned inside and the sign had been put up, the shutters of the store were pulled down.

Singh reached into his bag and pulled out a bunch of polythene bags and slips bearing government seals. As he distributed the bags to his officers, Singh said, 'Prakash*ji,* we will go around the shop and collect assorted samples of jewellery, which we will test in our labs for purity. You, as well as members of your staff, will accompany us around the shop as we collect these samples.'

Zaveri nodded, heavily perspiring even inside the air-conditioned store.

Singh turned towards the recruits, most of whom now had the plastic bags and the slips with government seals in their hands. 'Pick up samples and put them in the plastic bags. Then seal those bags, and staple the slips on them.'

Singh's words worked like magic. Harish felt a rush of power as his self-doubt and apprehensions vanished. Mohan*ji's* towering personality and his no-nonsense attitude seemed to have cast a spell on everyone around him. The way he had taken complete charge of the situation and seemed to be walking all over the staff and the owner of the store was something Harish had never witnessed before. There was so much to learn from that man!

Singh turned back towards Zaveri and said, 'You will need to hand over the cash you have at the counter. I will make out a receipt for the same. I will also need details of sales over the last year. Do you understand?'

Zaveri nodded again, wiping the sweat off his face.

In the next half hour, Singh and his men went around the showcases, accompanied by Zaveri and his staff. They picked up samples of jewellery that were packed in the plastic bags and sealed as Zaveri looked on helplessly.

Harish went about his job enthusiastically, beginning to enjoy the control he now exercised on a member of the staff who accompanied him and meekly handed over the samples of jewellery Harish demanded.

When the money had been collected, and samples of jewellery had been picked up from the showcases, the team started to load them into the briefcases that Singh had asked the recruits to bring along from the bus.

'Once you are done, I want two of you to load the briefcases onto the bus,' Singh instructed his officers, looking at his watch. It had been about forty-five minutes.

Harish and one of the other recruits, Raghav, started loading the briefcases onto the bus. Once they were done, they returned to the store and waited for further instructions.

Singh gestured at the recruits to assemble in a group. He stood at an arm's length from them, with his legs apart and his hands on his waist. He lowered his voice and spoke with steely resolve, 'I want you to stay in this store and keep watch. I need to supervise another raid in this area. By now, you must have learnt a thing or two about how you should conduct yourself in the field. We have them in our grip, and I want each one of you to make sure that we do not loosen our hold on them at any cost. I will be back once the other business has been taken care of. Am I clear?'

The officers nodded.

'Well done, gentlemen! Now hold the fort till I return,' Mohan Singh said and then walked out of the store with brisk steps in the direction of the bus.

Harish and the other officers stood with their jaws clenched and arms folded. The battlefield was now theirs.

***

An hour had passed since Mohan Singh had left on the bus.

The customers inside the store were getting restless. Some of them had children who had started bawling. Zaveri and his staff were beginning to raise their voices. Hungry and exhausted, Harish realised that the rookie officers were fast losing control of the situation. They were getting increasingly anxious about Mohan Singh's prolonged absence from the scene and were uncertain about their next step. Empty threats would no longer pass muster with the people inside the store.

Finally, Prakash Zaveri stepped forward and took matters into his hands.

'Call the DB Marg Police Station,' he ordered a member of his staff.

Harish could feel his knees give way. The world around him was a blur. As he collapsed on the ground, *Aai's* face flashed before his eyes. She must be waiting for her son to return home, dying to hear about his experience on the first day of working for the CBI.

***

Mohan Singh reclined in his seat inside the taxi and heaved a sigh of relief.

It had been a long journey, and he had finally made it!

Mohan Singh had put in an advertisement in *The Times of India* a few months ago in October 1986, inviting eligible candidates for the positions of Intelligence Officers and Security Officers in the CBI. To his surprise, more than a hundred and fifty candidates had turned up at the Taj Hotel for the interview. He had not interviewed anyone then, as it was a 'dress rehearsal' for what he was planning to do a few months later. Mohan Singh wondered what had induced so many men, including those who were already working, to appear for the interview. Was it the lure of a secure job with a good salary and societal respect or was it the zeal to serve the nation by investigating complex and sensitive cases of national importance?

This time, his mission had started off on the wrong foot, with the hotel not allowing him to conduct interviews in Room no. 415, where he had been staying. He, therefore, had had to hire an office at Mittal Towers in Nariman Point. The hotel, at least, had agreed to redirect the candidates to his office for the interview, since the advertisement had already been sent to the newspaper, inviting eligible candidates to the hotel.

Lady Luck had, thereafter, been on his side. The interviews had been conducted smoothly, and twenty-six young men had been brought on board for his 'operation'. The luxury coach had been hired through the Taj, and the unsuspecting men had been taken to the Opera House branch of Tribhovandas Bhimji Zaveri & Sons Jewellers. The 'raid' had progressed just as smoothly as he had planned. The fake CBI identity cards with the fake government insignia, the fake search warrant, the fake seizure slips with the government seal, and above all, his impeccable performance as a rough and tough CBI official had managed to fool everyone. Maybe he should have pursued a career in Bollywood! He would have given stiff competition to the ruling star of the day, Amitabh Bachchan.

Mohan Singh had taken the bus to the hotel, carrying with him the briefcases loaded with cash and jewellery. By his estimate, the loot would be worth anything between thirty and thirty-five lakhs of rupees.

At the hotel, Mohan had showered and changed into casual clothing. He had checked out and asked the bellboy to call a taxi. The boy had called a taxi from the nearby stand. Mohan had smiled to himself when the bellboy had courteously loaded the bags into the boot of the taxi.

Now sitting relaxed in the back seat of the taxi, Mohan congratulated himself on a job well done.

He looked out of the window. They had reached Vile Parle.

'Stop, I will need to get down here,' Mohan told the taxi driver. The bellboy had called the taxi from the stand near the hotel. The police would find the taxi driver easily and be able to track his movements. He had to leave the taxi as soon as possible.

He paid the fare, adding a tip, and asked the taxi driver to help him with the bags.

He then headed towards the auto stand.

***

Arvind Inamdar received a phone call at his office in the Police Headquarters in Mumbai on the afternoon of March 19, 1987. Inamdar, who would eventually retire in 2000 as the Director General of Police for Maharashtra, was in the crime division at that time.

The call was about a CBI raid that had taken place some time back in the Opera House store of Tribhovandas Bhimji Zaveri & Sons, one of the most prestigious jewellers of the time. Inamdar was told that the CBI officers had walked into the store, pulled the shutters down, ordered the customers and the staff to wait, and taken the registers. None of this sounded unusual to Inamdar. However, what he heard next made him sit up.

'They have seized a lot of jewellery, and one of them has decamped with all the jewellery and cash.'

That was unusual.

Police interrogation of the new 'recruits' led them to the Taj Intercontinental Hotel. Inquiries at the hotel revealed that Singh had mentioned that he was from Trivandrum, had stayed in Room no. 415, had wanted to use the room for conducting interviews for the CBI, and had been asked to conduct the interviews elsewhere, which he proceeded to do at Mittal Towers in Nariman Point, where the candidates had been redirected.

The police also came to know that Singh had checked out of the hotel shortly after the robbery at the store. The police spoke to the bellboy who had called a taxi for the departing guest. After conducting inquiries at the taxi stand, the police, with the help of the bellboy, readily identified the driver who had picked up Singh at the hotel. The taxi driver informed the police that he had dropped Singh at Vile Parle.

That was where the trail went cold. The police could find no one who had seen Singh after that.

The police promptly put out a nationwide alert.

Since Singh had mentioned that he hailed from Trivandrum, the police sent a team there. Based on some leads that the team managed to gather in Trivandrum, the police arrested a man named George Augustine Fernandes on the suspicion that he was the man they were looking for, but it soon turned out that George was a petty thief and not the man who had planned and executed the perfect heist at Tribhovandas Bhimji Zaveri.

In Mumbai, the police alerted their network of informers to check if the perpetrator belonged to one of the gangs operating in the city at that time, but that line of investigation did not lead anywhere.

Around the same time, a theory gained credence that the wanted man was a CBI officer who had gone rogue. The theory seemed likely because the man obviously was familiar with the ways of working of the CBI, and, based on what the police heard from eyewitnesses, his confidence and flamboyance seemed genuine. Inamdar worked with the CBI, checking records and interviewing several officials, and eventually ruled out the possibility.

There were rumours that the man might have escaped to Dubai. Deciding to leave no stone unturned, the police dispatched a team there as well. The team worked with the local police but returned empty-handed once again.

The man had acted alone without involving any accomplices. He had carefully erased all traces and seemed to have simply vanished into thin air with the loot. According to a report published in the same year, he had looted three lakhs and seventy-five thousand rupees in cash and jewellery worth about twenty lakhs. Other conflicting reports mentioned the heist amount to be between thirty and thirty-five lakh rupees. With an average annual inflation rate of 7.19 per cent between 1987 and 2024, an amount of thirty-five lakh rupees in 1987 is equivalent to more than four and a half crores in 2024.

The heist piqued the interest of the nation, and people from different parts of the country kept discussing it for months afterwards. While the failure to capture the con artist did hurt the investigating team, there was also reluctant and silent admiration for his style.

The police hoped that the man would surely try to pull off such a grand heist once again, and the next time, the police would be better prepared. However, none of that happened.

There is also a possibility that the man did pull off more heists, but they were flawless and went undetected. Alternately, he might have carefully chosen victims who had skeletons in their own cupboards and so, never reported the heists to the police.

The sensational robbery continued to make headlines for years, but the identity of the man who called himself Mohan Singh remained a mystery. Twenty-six years later, the exploits of the enigmatic man, who assembled a team of twenty-six other men, convincing them that they were working for the CBI, and carried out a daring heist in one of the busiest areas of South Bombay in broad daylight, became the inspiration behind a popular Bollywood movie.

The Great Train Robbery

Mohar Singh sighed and turned to his side as a train sped by his makeshift tent by the tracks with a deafening hoot, making the tent shake, like the trains did throughout the night, every night. He looked at the wristwatch he kept next to the pillow. It was past three in the morning, and he could not sleep. It was not the trains passing by or the dogs raising a ruckus over leftovers near the garbage bin close to his tent. In fact, he had become so accustomed to the sound of wheels on the tracks all night that he often wondered if he would manage to get any sleep at all in quieter surroundings, once the job was over and they left the place.

Mohar realised that it was the anticipation of what the next night had in store that had been fanning the fire in his heart and not letting his nerves calm down all through the night. He got up and took a sip of water from the plastic jug. Going back to bed, he closed his eyes again, hoping he would finally get some sleep.

Tomorrow was a big day, and he could not afford to feel groggy all day. He wondered if the others were also awake.

***

Mohar Singh, along with the Pardis—Dinesh, Rohan, Rusi, Mahesh, Kaliya, and Brajmohan—had arrived in the area some time back. There was a construction site close by, and they had easily managed to take up jobs as daily wage workers there. They had put up tents along the Salem-Chennai railway track, near the station and under the overbridge. This was a common practice among many of the labourers who worked in the area. No one seemed to mind.

Before long, they had got used to scenes of teeming crowds on the nearby platform, the rundown shanties on both sides of the tracks, scantily clad kids playing around, dogs scavenging for food in the garbage, women indifferently going about their chores all day long, and men, mostly in disreputable professions, returning home late in the nights, high on cheap country liquor or *ganja*, and raising a ruckus.

This was not new for the members of the tribe. They have always been known for spreading out across different parts of the country, such as Madhya Pradesh, Rajasthan, Delhi, Haryana, Gujarat, and Maharashtra, staying on roadsides or along railway tracks, working as daily wage earners or selling toys and balloons, on the lookout for opportunities.

Mohar Singh had a long history of sophisticated and large-scale criminal activities. Starting his career with small thefts and burglaries in his native Gaya district in Bihar, Mohar Singh graduated to organised crime, forming and leading a gang that specialised in large-scale robberies targeting trains, warehouses, and financial institutions across several states, including Rajasthan, Delhi, Gujarat, and Maharashtra. Singh built a strong network of informants and collaborators, which included insiders in target organisations. This network provided critical intelligence, making his heists more effective. He also reportedly had connections with other criminal syndicates, helping him procure sophisticated tools and evade law enforcement agencies for extended periods.

In 2012, Mohar Singh and his gang were implicated in a robbery in a passenger train in the Eastern Railway zone, where cash and valuables were stolen from locked compartments. The gang targeted specific compartments based on insider information and breached the compartments by dismantling locks during a planned stop in a remote location. In 2014, Singh's gang broke into a bank in Gaya, Bihar, and looted one crore and twenty lakhs in cash and gold jewellery from lockers. They used gas cutters and specialised tools to break through the vault, likely working overnight. In 2015, the gang targeted a prominent jewellery shop in a small town in Uttar Pradesh, stealing approximately eighty lakhs worth of gold and diamonds. Posing as customers during the day, the gang scoped the shop's layout and security measures. Later, they drilled through a wall to gain entry and looted the showroom.

While the heists designed by Mohar Singh were characterised by their ingenuity, they were not always devoid of violence. In many cases, Singh and his gang were known to use intimidation and, in some cases, armed force, to subdue resistance during their operations.

***

One evening, a few months ago, Mohar's gang assembled inside his dimly lit tent. There was a musty odour inside, and it was quite normal to feel a mouse scamper across one's feet.

'I have news from a friend in Salem,' Mohar said. There seemed to be, finally, an opportunity in sight, something that would justify the miserable life the members of the gang had been living for months by that railway track.

Kaliya smiled and looked at the others. He said, 'Boss has friends in all the right places, doesn't he?'

His comment was met with uproarious laughter across the tent. Every time Mohar had a plan, he began his speech with the exact same words, barring the location, which changed every time.

'Brothers, let us be serious, please,' said Mohar, sounding very business-like.

The laughter died down almost immediately.

'There is going to be movement of a lot of money along the Salem-Chennai train route very soon,' Mohar said, looking into the eyes of each member of the gang who was now listening to him attentively. 'I have been told that a large amount of money will be transferred between banks on this route. We need to get our hands on the cash.'

No one spoke inside the tent for some time. Rusi was the first to break the silence. He said, 'This sounds like a great idea, but I am sure there will be tight security on the train. They must be having armed guards. I don't think we will be able to put up a fight.'

Mahesh said, 'Forget about putting up a fight. How do we even break in?'

Mohar said, 'You are right. I am sure security will be beefed up, and it will not be easy to get to the money using conventional methods. We cannot just jump into the train, take on the guards with our *desi katta*-s, and overpower them. That is why we have to think outside the box. I have a plan, which may sound dangerous, maybe even unrealistic, but I am sure that if we prepare ourselves well enough, there is no reason why we should not succeed.' He paused for a while and looked at every member of the gang, his eyes shining in the dim light inside the shack. 'Trust me, if we manage to pull this off, our names will go down in history.'

'What is your plan?' asked Rusi, sounding impatient.

Mohar smiled and said, 'We will enter the coach through the roof.'

***

The train carrying the money was to travel from Salem to Chennai Egmore railway station. Over the next few months, the gang members took turns to travel in trains along the route for conducting the essential reconnaissance.

They realised early on that in order to break into a coach of the train through the roof, they would need to very quickly cut a hole, wide enough to allow a person to pass through. The hole had to be cut while standing on top of a moving train.

The biggest obstacle to the process would be the overhead high tension electric wires carrying twenty-five thousand volts. It tuned out that the segment of the route till Virudhachalam had not been electrified yet while that from Virudhachalam till Chennai Egmore had been completely electrified. As such, the engine of the train would change from a diesel locomotive one to an electric locomotive one at Virudhachalam. It was, therefore, decided that the robbery would have to be carried out before the train reached Virudhachalam.

The gang members travelled between Ayothiapattinam, a panchayat town in Salem district, and Virudhachalam for more than a week, trying to identify the segment of the route that was most suitable for carrying out their plan. The ideal segment would be one where the train did not halt and allowed sufficient time for the necessary activities to be carried out. It turned out that the segment of the route between Chinnasalem and Virudhachalam would be appropriate, as the train ran in that stretch for more than forty-five minutes without stopping.

Before long, the gang had the plan ready. Over the next few weeks, they procured the essential tools. Mohar Singh was constantly in touch with his friend in Salem. Finally, he received confirmation that the train would start from Salem Junction on the night of August 8, 2016. Mohar Singh got the gang together and walked them through the plan down to the most minute details once again.

It was now just a matter of time before the gang struck gold.

***

The Salem-Chennai Egmore Express started from Salem Junction at five minutes past nine on the night of August 8.

The train was carrying soiled currency notes with a face value of more than three hundred and forty crores of rupees. The money was being transferred from branches of the Indian Overseas Bank in Salem and two other locations to the Reserve Bank of India.

The money had been packed into two hundred and twenty-six wooden boxes. The boxes had then been loaded into a heavy parcel van (VPH) that is traditionally used to transport cargo in Indian Railways. The van, numbered VPH 08831, itself had been sealed.

The consignment was being transported under high security. A police team led by an Assistant Commissioner had been deployed. They had spread out across different parts of the train. Fifteen RPF (Railway Police Force) personnel had also been deployed. They had been divided into two teams. Some of the RPF personnel had been posted in the GC (general compartment) of the train that was right before the parcel van to make sure that there was no movement from the GC in the direction of the VPH. The second team of RPF personnel was deployed in the Guard Coach that was attached behind the VPH. As such, there could be no movement into the VPH from the direction of the engine and the Guard Coach as well.

Having thus secured the entrances to the parcel van on both sides, no one had thought of deploying security personnel inside the van itself.

***

At Chinnasalem railway platform, silence prevailed, punctuated by the occasional hum of a passing train or the distant bark of dogs. Dim yellow lights from the platform cast a faint glow on the surrounding area, creating long, soft shadows of a few scattered trees. The platform was modest, with only a handful of travellers seated on wooden benches, waiting for late-night trains.

Beyond the platform, the surroundings, with clusters of small houses and shops that had closed for the night a long time back, melted into the darkness. The August air was cool, carrying faint earthy and floral scents from nearby fields and gardens. Streetlights flickered occasionally, their pale beams illuminating patches of the adjoining roads.

The faint buzz of insects and the chirping of crickets were the only sounds that could be heard. Occasionally, a two-wheeler or a rickety auto rickshaw would pass by on the road near the station, the sound of its engine breaking the stillness briefly before fading into the distance.

As the Salem-Chennai Egmore Express rolled into the station, five men, who had been hiding inconspicuously in the darkness some distance away from the platform, came out of the shadows. When the train started moving after a brief halt, the men began to run alongside with long strides. As the train picked up speed, no one noticed when Mohar Singh and four members of the gang jumped onto the train in the cover of darkness.

In no time, the five men made their way to the roof of a passenger coach, not far from the parcel van, which was their coveted destination. Thankfully, the weather gods had been kind, relieving them of one of their biggest worries about rains ruining their plans. Five shadows against the ink-black sky made their way towards the parcel van, the wind in their faces making it difficult to keep their eyes open. The air was heavy with the damp aroma of woods and open fields that lined the railway tracks, which glistened in the moonlight, twisting and turning like a gigantic snake as far as the eye could see.

The five men lost no time.

They pulled out the cutters they had been carrying—some of them battery-operated, some manual. As they started cutting a hole in the roof of the parcel van, the wind roared in their ears and the relentless drumming of the wheels on the railway tracks reverberated in the stillness of the night.

Before long, they cut a hole two to three feet wide, wide enough for them to lower themselves into the parcel van. As they had planned, two of them entered the van, while three remained on the roof. Mohar Singh monitored the time on the radium-lit dial of his wristwatch and barked orders.

The two men inside the van saw wooden boxes piled all around them. They had less than half an hour to finish the job. They immediately realised that there was no way they could open all the boxes before the train reached Virudhachalam, where, as per Mohar Singh's instructions, they were to get off the train. They would have to be content with whatever they could grab in the short time.

With bated breath, they got down to work right away. Their hands shaking in excitement and sweat streaming down their bodies, the two started breaking the boxes open and stuffing the money into *lungi*-s that they were carrying. They had to take extra care that the noise from their movements inside the van and the breaking of the wooden boxes did not rise above the clamour of the wheels.

'If the guards are not inside the parcel van itself, then they must be in the adjoining coaches,' Mohar Singh had warned them before they entered the van.

Mohar Singh kept looking around, as the train rushed through the rural heartland of Tamil Nadu, its rhythmic clatter filling the air, blending with the occasional horn that echoed in the quiet night. Paddy fields stretched into the horizon, their waterlogged surfaces reflecting the night sky. Dotted along the route were small villages, their homes dimly lit by kerosene lamps. Occasionally, temple spires rose from the horizon. Groves of tamarind and coconut trees lined the tracks at intervals, their swaying leaves whispering in the night air.

By the time the two men inside the parcel van had filled up six *lungi*-s, they heard Mohar Singh's voice from the roof above the howl of the wind, 'Wind up now! We are approaching the overbridge!'

The train was nearing Virudhachalam. Mohar Singh could see from a distance the signs of a larger town—scattered streetlights on distant roads and clusters of houses more densely packed.

The two men looked regretfully at the boxes they had not managed to open and wondered if they could have gone about their job any faster. They handed the *lungi*-s over to the men on the roof through the hole. Then, looking at the unopened boxes around the van one last time and shaking their heads in regret, they climbed up on the boxes. They supported themselves on their hands on the two sides of the hole and pulled themselves up, one after the other, with help from the men on the roof.

When they reached the roof of the van, the cold air of the night caressed them and the two finally breathed freely. Mohar Singh patted them on their backs.

The rest of the gang, led by Mahesh Pardi, was waiting by the side of the railway track under the Vayalur overbridge, close to the Virudhachalam railway station. As the train approached the overbridge, the men on the train began to throw the cash packed in six *lungi*-s by the tracks.

The train slowed down as it approached the Virudhachalam station. The five men climbed down from the roof of the parcel van and jumped off the train. They met their partners waiting under the overbridge, who, by that time, had gathered the loot. It was later estimated that they had managed to steal a little less than six crores of rupees from the van.

'We did it!' roared Mohar Singh, tears of joy in his eyes. The jubilant men huddled together and hugged each other. What they had pulled off a while back was no less than what trained stuntmen did in Bollywood movies after weeks of planning and rehearsals with state-of-the-art security measures. Only this time, the smell of money was real!

The train reached the Virudhachalam station at ten minutes to twelve and left at a quarter past twelve, after an electric engine had been substituted for its diesel engine.

By that time, the men had vanished into the night.

***

The Salem-Chennai Egmore Express arrived at the Egmore station at five minutes to four the next morning. The security personnel disembarked. The parcel van remained sealed. It was to be opened only after the arrival of the Reserve Bank of India officials.

The Reserve Bank of India officials arrived at the Egmore station at eleven on the morning of August 9. The parcel van was opened.

No one was ready for the sight that greeted them. In the bright daylight that beamed into the van through a gaping hole in the roof, the officials saw that the wooden boxes lay scattered around. Stupefied, they stepped into the van. They saw that a total of four boxes had been broken. One of the boxes was empty, with all the cash missing. Two more were more than half-empty. Another box had been opened, but the money inside was just scattered. The reason could be that the box had currency notes of comparatively smaller denominations.

The security personnel on duty inside the train were immediately summoned. None of them had a clue regarding what had happened inside the van the previous night. Since the guards had been deployed either in the adjoining general coach for passengers or in the Guard Coach next to the van, they had neither seen nor heard the intruders.

'We have seen this happen only in movies!' one of the policemen commented, his eyes fixed on the hole in the roof.

The matter was immediately reported to the Government Railway Police, and an elaborate investigation was initiated. The forensics team arrived at the spot in no time. They collected evidence from the van. These included fingerprints on the boxes and walls of the van. They also found shreds of clothing that had been torn away.

The police stations along the route from Salem to Chennai were alerted. Inspectors from all those stations were roped in. They were instructed to conduct thorough searches in their respective areas of jurisdiction and also check for suspicious movements in those areas over the last few days.

This was most certainly the work of professional robbers, who were adept at such daring acts. They must have had detailed information about the consignment, as well as the route and timings of the train. Some of the investigators suggested that insiders from the Railways might have been involved. How else could the robbers have information about the money being transported? How else would they know the best time and the best segment of the route to carry out the daring robbery inside a moving train and then decamp with the money undetected?

As expected, the sensational robbery drew its share of media attention. Two days later, on August 11, 2016, the case was handed over to the Crime Branch of the CID in Tamil Nadu. However, for months together, the detectives were at their wits' end, trying to figure out how the dramatic robbery had been planned and executed and who the perpetrators were. There were no eyewitnesses. Forensic evidence did not take them far. Police operations in the areas surrounding the route did not yield results, either.

The Crime Branch CID officials then decided to cast a wider net. They deployed informants in different parts of the country to gather information about gangs that operated across states. A special team was formed that travelled across the length and breadth of the country to collect intelligence and interrogate potential suspects. The police also visited places like construction sites and mines where soiled currency notes are often used in transactions. Since the numbers of the missing notes had already been circulated throughout the country, it was unlikely that the robbers would use any of the conventional channels for exchanging soiled currency notes, like the Reserve Bank of India, public sector banks, or the currency chest branches of private sector banks.

After nearly two years of investigation, there was light at the end of the tunnel. Officers visiting the state of Madhya Pradesh spoke to policemen in the Ujjain and Guna districts and came to know about gangs in MP that operated across states. Using technical inputs like call data records and tower locations of the mobile phones belonging to the members of these gangs, the police began to piece together information on the suspects.

The police received information that two of the gang members were on a visit to Chennai. Eventually, on October 12, 2018, two men, Dinesh Pardi and Rohan Pardi, both residents of Ratlam, Madhya Pradesh, were arrested in Chennai.

On interrogation, the two confessed that they had been part of a gang that had committed the daring robbery in the Salem-Chennai Egmore Express on the night of August 8, 2016. They revealed the names of other members of the gang and mentioned that the operation had been led by Mohar Singh, who belonged to a group of Pardi criminals that committed such crimes in various states across the country. The police found out that the other perpetrators, including Mohar Singh, were lodged in various prisons in Madhya Pradesh, where they had been arrested for their involvement in other crimes.

On October 30, 2018, the police brought the other five—Rusi, Mahesh, Kaliya, and Brajmohan along with their leader, Mohar Singh—to a Chennai court on prisoner transit warrant. Mohar, Rusi, Kaliya, and Mahesh had been taken into custody from the Central Prison in Guna district, while Brajmohan had been moved from the Ashok Nagar prison.

All the gang members confessed to the crime during the police investigation. Further interrogation, aimed at the recovery of the stolen money, led to a shocking discovery.

As destiny would have it, on November 8, 2016, three months after the daring heist, demonetisation of Rs. 500 and Rs. 1000 banknotes was announced in India. By then, most of the gang members had already purchased immovable property with some of the money. What remained of the loot was rendered useless by the announcement of demonetisation. The robbers, with tears in their eyes, burnt about a third of the loot, worth nearly two crores of rupees, and threw away the rest into rivers.

The Loot at the End of the Tunnel

'Boys,' Mahipal addressed the young men assembled in the room, 'our time has come. It's time to think big!'

Satish, Surender, Balraj, and Rajesh looked at each other. They were all aged around thirty years and hailed from Katwal, a village in the Sonepat district of Haryana. They then turned towards Mahipal, wanting to hear what brilliant idea brewed in his fertile mind.

Mahipal was fifty-three years old and had a son and three daughters. He had, over the years, tried his luck in several business ventures. He had driven taxis and run a motel, before finally settling for the real estate business. He dealt mostly in disputed properties. His friends believed that Mahipal's brain worked like a computer.

From his early days of earning a meagre salary of seven hundred rupees a month driving taxis, he now owned a taxi stand, multi-storey buildings, and a house in the village.

Keen to make some fast cash, Mahipal had hit upon a grand idea about six months back, but he needed to assemble a team for its successful execution. Satish, his partner in the property business, who was single and stayed with his mother in Katwal village, had come to his help. He was in dire need of money and had told Mahipal that he was ready to do anything to that end. He had offered to bring his friends from the village along to meet Mahipal. All of them were down on their luck and would be happy to execute Mahipal's plan.

The ones who had readily agreed to meet Mahipal were Balraj, Surender, and Rajesh.

Balraj was single and worked with his father as a farmer. Surender was a father of two and lived with his parents and wife. Coming from a family of carpenters, Surender ran a small pathological laboratory outside the Government Medical College for Women. He did not own land and was cash-strapped, and the laboratory was not doing well either. Rajesh had lost his father and lived with his mother. He had had to sell off his land to build a house. He was the only one in the group who had a criminal record. A case under the Narcotic Drugs and Psychotropic Substances Act had been registered against him in Himachal Pradesh five years ago, and another case related to a criminal conspiracy under Section 120-B had been registered at the Gohana Sadar Police Station three years ago. But those cases had not daunted his spirits in any way.

Satish spoke on behalf of the group of boys, 'Mahipal*ji*, what's the plan?'

'We will rob a bank!' Mahipal declared, reclining in his chair.

For the next hour, everyone listened to Mahipal in rapt attention.

***

The branch of Punjab National Bank in Sonepat district, which Mahipal had set his eyes on, was in the residential-cum-commercial town of Gohana.

Back in 2014, the town of Gohana was in transition, balancing its traditional rural roots with the aspirations of modernisation and development, reflecting the broader socio-economic changes occurring across Haryana. Located about thirty-five kilometres from the district headquarters, Sonepat, and approximately sixty kilometres from Delhi, Gohana was well-connected via road, with state highways linking it to major cities in Haryana and neighbouring states. The economy was predominantly agricultural, with many residents engaged in farming, particularly in wheat, rice, and sugarcane cultivation. There was a grain market (*mandi*) that served as a trade centre for local farmers. At the same time, there were emerging small-scale industries, shops, and businesses contributing to the urbanisation of the town. Growing urbanisation brought development, such as better roads, new markets, and residential colonies.

All these factors made the particular branch of Punjab National Bank, which Mahipal had targeted, rather important both for individuals and families, as well as for businesses around the area.

'I have a locker in the bank, which has allowed me to perform a thorough reconnaissance of the bank and its surroundings. I have a crystal-clear understanding of the layout of the bank, the location of the lockers, as well as the security measures in place,' Mahipal had told his team in the first meeting.

Egged on by Mahipal, in the subsequent months, the young men also took part in the reconnaissance of the bank and its surroundings. Confident that they had gathered enough information about the layout of the bank and the security measures, the gang believed that they were ready to break in. Thereafter, they made two unsuccessful attempts to enter the bank unnoticed—once from the rear side of the building and on another occasion, from the roof. They soon realised that they had to devise a smarter way of getting inside the bank.

It was then that Mahipal hit upon a brilliant idea. He assembled his team and discussed his idea with them.

'I have an abandoned house right opposite the bank. It is a disputed property and has been lying vacant for the past five years. As a part of my reconnaissance of the bank, I have measured the distance between the house and the bank across the road in the old-fashioned way—using footsteps,' Mahipal smiled. The four men kept looking at him, their eyes wide in wonder.

Mahipal continued, 'You must have noticed that the strongroom where the lockers are present is at the extreme end of the building. Also, the floor of the strongroom is at least two to three feet below the ground level. There are no steel plates on the floor of the room, like many other banks do. There is no CCTV camera inside, as the bank authorities here feel that it is not appropriate to have surveillance inside the strongroom, where customers should be allowed privacy.'

Mahipal paused for effect. The men kept wondering what the sly old fox was up to.

'So, what's the plan?' Rajesh sounded restless.

'What if we dig a tunnel from the abandoned house that opens in the strongroom and enter the bank through that route?' Mahipal asked, looking into the eyes of each one of the men.

It was as if a bomb had exploded inside the room, rendering everyone speechless. The four men looked at each other. The plan, though theoretically plausible, sounded fantastic when viewed through the lens of practicality.

'It sounds like a great idea, Mahipal*ji*,' mumbled Satish after he had recovered somewhat from the shock induced by Mahipal's proposition, 'but how can we dig a tunnel right across the road, which must be more than eighty feet in width?'

'And how do we dig it without getting caught?' asked Balraj. 'We've never done anything like that!' he added.

'There is a first time for everything, Balraj. There is nothing that cannot be achieved if you put your heart and soul and your brain into it,' smiled Mahipal. 'We will find a way to get there.'

Once he had hit upon the idea, there was no stopping Mahipal.

He assembled his partners in crime and spent the next eight weeks chalking out an elaborate plan. The men could pose as tenants in the empty house and use it as their base. They could work from the house without questions being asked. After all, the house belonged to Mahipal himself.

The men immediately went about their business.

As the season was beginning to change from the warm monsoon to the onset of the pleasant autumn, nights in Gohana were becoming colder and quieter. The skies were mostly clear, with occasional traces of clouds. The town would start quieting down after nine or ten in the night, with markets and shops closing for the day. The only sounds that could be heard were the occasional sounds of crickets, barking dogs, and the horns of long-distance buses and trucks that passed through the highways near Gohana.

The young men would start digging the tunnel at night and work till dawn. They used iron rods, spades, and trowels for their work. Surender, coming from a family of carpenters, provided valuable recommendations about reinforcing the tunnel to prevent its collapse. The digging was done so perfectly that underground telephone lines and water pipelines were not damaged.

For these young men from a village in the back of beyond, every stone they moved, every barrier they broke through brought them closer to the realisation of their dream of a life of comfort and security for their families and themselves. Their debts would be paid off, their future would be secure, and there was life at the end of the tunnel. This dream kept them energised and invigorated all through the long cold nights as they kept digging. The secret of their audacious plan remained buried in the bowels of the Earth for weeks.

***

After forty nights, the tunnel was ready. It was eighty-four feet long and was about six feet under the ground. It was about three feet high and about two and a half feet wide.

The grand heist was planned on the intervening night of October 26 and 27, 2014. The previous night was the intervening night between a Saturday and a Sunday. With the bank being closed over the weekend, the digging of the last segment of the tunnel had gone undetected.

On the night of October 26, when Satish, Balraj, Surender, and Rajesh assembled in the dilapidated building, there was an eerie silence all around. The men slipped into the tunnel one after the other, carrying lanterns and sacks, and headed towards the strongroom, their hearts drumming against their ribs. The next few moments were going to change the course of their lives for good.

After what seemed like an endless trek down the tunnel, the men finally reached the end. Satish led the pack. With a tearing sound, he turned a wide stone over upon its side, leaving a square gaping hole in the floor of the room. He turned towards his mates.

'*Khul ja sim sim!*' he said with a wink.

The men following him, their faces sweaty and murky yet beaming in the faint light of the lanterns inside the tunnel, chuckled and repeated his words in unison, '*Khul ja sim sim!*'

Satish peeped over the edge of the hole and looked around inside the room, raising his lantern. Then, with a hand on either side of the hole, he pulled himself up gradually—first shoulder-high and then waist-high. Then, he had a knee upon the edge, and in the next moment, he stood at the side of the hole inside the strongroom. He stretched his hand out and started pulling his companions up one after the other.

The four audacious men had finally broken into the strongroom of the bank.

Once inside, they felt like kids in a candy store. The strongroom had three hundred and fifty lockers, which were now for them to plunder. The lockers themselves were sixty to seventy years old and could be opened easily with jacks and steel cutters, which the men lost no time in pulling out of the sacks they were carrying.

Over the next six hours till dawn, the four men filled up two sacks and their own pockets with jewellery, cash, and other valuables (which were later estimated to be worth more than a hundred crores). By the time it was dawn and time for the men to retrace their way to the house down the tunnel, they had managed to empty as many as eighty-nine lockers.

When they finally crawled out of the tunnel into the empty house, the men were jubilant, their eyes filled with dreams of a new life of affluence, which, till a few days ago, had seemed unattainable. The men distributed the booty among them and walked out of the house. A bright new day awaited them.

The robbery was detected later in the day.

When a customer went inside the strongroom to operate his locker, he was greeted by the shocking sight of empty lockers all around, some with broken locks still dangling from them. The customer raised an alarm. The manager, Devender Malik, immediately called the police.

***

Haryana Police started the investigation with the highest priority, especially because the heist had created such a sensation that a top-ranking official from the Prime Minister's Office had been dispatched to the site to assess the situation on the ground and report back.

The tunnel itself led the police to the house from where it had been dug. The police gathered crucial forensic evidence, including soil samples, fingerprints, and pieces of clothing among others, from the tunnel and the abandoned house where the tunnel originated. The police carried out extensive interrogation of residents and shop owners in the neighbourhood of the house, hoping to gather information about suspicious activities they might have noticed inside and around the house in the last few weeks. Some of the local residents and shopkeepers mentioned four men visiting the house at odd hours. They also provided descriptions of those men, who had claimed that they had rented the house. While the location of the house itself was such that it managed to escape any CCTV surveillance, footage from cameras at the neighbouring roads and crossings revealed suspicious movements of those men moving towards or away from the dilapidated house that had suddenly become the centre of attention in the town.

The Haryana DGP, in the meantime, announced a reward of ten lakh rupees for anyone who could provide relevant information regarding the heist. The police also formed seven teams to carry out investigations in the twenty-odd big villages that surrounded the town of Gohana. The police started inquiries in the villages, trying to find out if the villagers had noticed a group of young men missing from the village for more than a month.

Back in Gohana, the police found their first productive clues from the plywood boards that the robbers had used to cover the windows of the house. On careful scrutiny, the police found that the name and the address of the shop from where the boards had been purchased were imprinted on them. The police immediately contacted the shopkeeper. Inquiries at the shop led the police to Mahipal, who also turned out to be the man who owned the house in question. Mahipal was immediately summoned for questioning.

'I know nothing about the robbery,' Mahipal feigned ignorance. 'Four men had, indeed, rented the house from me, but I did not have the slightest idea of what they were up to!' Mahipal told the police.

'When was the last time you had visited the house?' asked the Superintendent of Police (SP) in charge of the investigation.

'I haven't been to the house in a long time,' claimed Mahipal.

This raised suspicion in the mind of the SP. He called one of his officers aside and said, 'That man is lying!'

'What makes you think so, Sir?' asked the officer, baffled.

The SP replied, 'It was Diwali a few days ago. It is our tradition to light *diyas* and dispel darkness from our houses during Diwali. It is unlikely that someone who lived a stone's throw away did not visit and illuminate the house. Check with the neighbours. I am sure many of them would have seen the house lit up on Diwali. Why is

Mahipal lying? Let him go, but put him under surveillance. Check his call records.'

During the next few hours, the police found out from the neighbours that they had, indeed, seen the house lit up on Diwali. This revelation added credence to the SP's theory that Mahipal was lying. His call records revealed that he had contacted a couple of numbers several times over the last few months. It turned out that the numbers most frequently connected with belonged to two men—Satish and Rajesh.

Around the same time, the SP received a call from Jaspal Singh, the officer leading a police team that was conducting inquiries in Katwal.

'Sir, I have an update,' Jaspal sounded excited at the other end of the line.

'What is it, Jaspal?' the SP asked.

'Sir, villagers here in Katwal have told us that there are four men—Satish, Surender, Balraj, and Rajesh—whom they have not seen for the last few months. They told us that Satish works in Gohana in a company dealing in properties. I think he could be connected to Mahipal. These could be the men we are looking for. I have a local informer who tells me that two of them have recently returned to the village,' said Jaspal.

The SP was already gesturing at an officer to prepare for a mission. The team moved quickly.

On the night of October 30, the police surrounded the village of Katwal. The villagers had finished dinner a while ago and had retired for the day. Some of them were watching television, while others had gone to bed. Suddenly, the silence of the night was shattered by the sounds of four-wheelers, accompanied by the wails of police sirens. The villagers came rushing out of their houses. In no time, the police were swarming over the streets. The residents of Katwal had never seen a police crackdown.

Before the new day dawned, the police had arrested Surender and Balraj from the village with the assistance of local informers. The police recovered about ten kilograms of jewellery from a bag they had hidden in a brick kiln in the village. Surender and Balraj confessed to the crime and mentioned the names of the others involved in the heist.

Back in Gohana, around the same time, the police intercepted a call received by Mahipal on his phone, which had been under surveillance. The caller was Satish, who had contacted Mahipal to check on the progress of the investigation. A police team was immediately sent to an outer colony of Gohana, from where Satish had called. He was also taken into custody. He confessed to the crime as well.

The next morning, Mahipal was summoned to the police station again for questioning. The police still did not have enough evidence to prove Mahipal's involvement in the heist. Mahipal maintained that he knew the men and had been in touch with some of them on the phone, but only as his tenants.

What happened thereafter is shrouded in mystery.

Mahipal's son, Rajkumar, said later that he had received a call from his father, asking to be picked up from the police station. However, when Rajkumar reached the station, he was told that his father had been told to go home unescorted. Mahipal had a problem with his right arm and, therefore, avoided driving. That morning, however, he had driven down to the police station on his own. After leaving the station, Mahipal called his family and informed them that he had been let off by the police as he was innocent. He told them that he had spoken to a business associate on the phone and had to attend an urgent meeting. Later, at around four that afternoon, the family received news that Mahipal had been found dead in his car on the Gohana-Panipat Highway.

The family rushed to the site.

The Gohana-Panipat Highway was a key roadway, connecting the town of Gohana to the city of Panipat. At the time, traffic was moderately busy, with a mix of commercial vehicles, private cars, motorbikes, tractors, and the occasional bullock carts. Trucks and goods carriers, transporting agricultural produce and industrial goods between Gohana, Panipat, and neighbouring areas, zoomed past, blowing their horns. The part of the highway where the car had been found was lined with trees and flanked by agricultural fields, with small villages and clusters of *dhabas* visible at a distance.

Mahipal's cousin, Abhimanyu, said that the car 'reeked of a noxious stench'. The lifeless body of the mastermind of the grand heist lay on the driver's seat, which was reclined. Mahipal's trousers were dirty, and there was no sign of a struggle. It seemed as if someone had placed his body on the seat.

The family contended that while Mahipal might have known the people who had rented his house and committed the heist, he had not been involved. They questioned who in his right mind would plan a heist by digging a tunnel from his own house that stood across the road from the bank and who himself lived a stone's throw away from the bank. Would it not automatically invite suspicion? On the question of the neighbours having seen lights in the dilapidated house on the night of Diwali, Rajkumar stated that it was he who had asked his father if he could put some lights up in that house. Mahipal had agreed, and Rajkumar had visited the house and placed *diyas* on the parapet wall. Mahipal had not gone to the house himself and had, therefore, told the police that he had not been to the house in a very long time. Rajkumar questioned why his father would allow him to step into the house if he had known that a tunnel was being dug from there to the strongroom of the bank across the road.

The family also questioned why the police had allowed Mahipal to leave the station unescorted. Had he been a suspect, would the police let him off? The family strongly contended that while Mahipal might have been distressed by the circumstances and ashamed of his name being connected with the heist, he was not the kind of person who would take his life.

The police, on the other hand, felt that Mahipal feared imminent arrest after learning that Satish had been taken into custody, and he committed suicide by consuming a poisonous substance.

Rajesh, the only seasoned criminal in the gang, was still at large.

***

'We feel that we have justified reasons to be furious. The bank has been housed in this building since 1983. The lockers are even older and could be opened easily by a bunch of rookies as they are worn out. The bank did not follow the practice of reinforcing the floor of the strongroom with metal sheets or thickening the concrete,' said one of the customers demonstrating in front of the bank. The customers also found it improbable that the four men and their mastermind performed a reconnaissance almost daily and entered the bank through a tunnel in the ground, without anyone in the bank being aware of the same for more than a month. Although the police records did not mention any possibility of one or more bank employees being involved in the heist, the agitated customers who had suffered heavy losses refused to believe the same. They lodged a police complaint against the officials of the bank. They demanded compensation from the bank.

The bank denied the allegation that the floor was not adequately thick. The bank officials, citing guidelines put in place by the Reserve Bank of India, refused to compensate the customers for the losses. The customers were told that the bank did not maintain records of what customers had placed in the lockers and was not liable.

***

Rajesh, the last of the accused, was arrested a few weeks later, on November 21, by a police team near the Bawana railway crossing in Narela, close to the Haryana border.

The police eventually recovered from the four arrested men about fifty kilograms of jewellery and four lakhs rupees in cash, along with a country-made pistol and two cartridges.

No recovery could be made from Mahipal's family after his death. When the police interrogated those arrested, it was learnt that they had shared the booty equally among themselves. Mahipal had instructed them to bring the jewellery to him after some time had lapsed. He would melt it into bars and sell it in the market. However, that was not to be. Destiny had other plans in store for the five men who had pulled off one of the most sensational bank robberies in the history of the nation.

This is the Prime Minister Speaking

May 24, 1971

It was about a quarter to twelve on a busy Monday morning in the Parliament Street branch of State Bank of India.

Ved Prakash Malhotra, the forty-six-year-old Chief Cashier, was in his office. He was in a meeting with an old and respected client of the bank. The conversation was interrupted by the ringing of one of the telephones on his desk—the one which had a direct number. Malhotra understood that the call had been made from outside the bank. He picked up the receiver. 'Hello, this is Ved Prakash Malhotra speaking,' he said.

'Hello, Mr. Malhotra. Shri P. N. Haksar, Principal Secretary to the Honourable Prime Minister of India, would like to talk to you.' There was a sense of urgency in the voice on the other side of the line, which was not lost on Malhotra.

Malhotra sat up straight, almost in reflex action. It was common knowledge that Parmeshwar Narayan Haksar was a reputed and respected bureaucrat and diplomat, who was not just Prime Minister Indira Gandhi's principal secretary but was also considered the chief strategist and policy adviser to the Prime Minister.

After a brief pause, a different voice on the line said, 'Hello, this is the Principal Secretary to the Honourable Prime Minister speaking.'

'Hello Sir, good morning,' Malhotra said, with reverence in his voice. 'How may I be of help?'

'Mr. Malhotra, there is a matter of utmost secrecy that I would like to discuss with you. Can you kindly confirm that you are alone inside your chamber?'

Malhotra looked at his client sitting across the table and hesitatingly gestured to be excused. After the client had left Malhotra's chamber, the latter returned to the call. 'I am alone in my cabin now,' Malhotra confirmed.

'Mr. Malhotra, let me come straight to the point. The matter is urgent, and we do not have time to lose. The Prime Minister of India wants sixty lakh rupees to be withdrawn from your bank for a task that is highly confidential in nature and is of utmost importance to the nation. That is the reason why I am speaking to you directly. You will need to hand over the money personally to a person we will send across for the purpose.' The instructions, albeit unexpected, were quick and unambiguous.

Malhotra had never felt more honoured and inspired in his entire life. There was an immediate surge of patriotic fervour in his heart. He bent forward, elbows resting on the table, and said, 'Sir, I will carry out your orders immediately. May I ask you if the money will be released against a cheque or a receipt?'

'Mr. Malhotra, as I told you, the matter is urgent. I request you to prioritise it and proceed. The formalities can be taken care of later. You will most certainly receive a cheque or a receipt,' the secretary sounded curt, even a bit annoyed. Malhotra wondered if he had offended him by asking a procedural question, which probably had been inappropriate under the circumstances.

In the meantime, further instructions were being given to Malhotra. 'The money will be sent to Bangladesh by a plane of the Indian Air Force. Therefore, you should bring the money to the Parliament Street Free Church. Let me repeat, the matter is highly confidential, and you must carry the cash yourself. Do you have any questions?'

Although Malhotra was still overwhelmed with a sense of self-importance, he was slowly beginning to realise that the demand was extraordinary. The amount of money involved was large, and a cheque or a money receipt was not available, at least for the time being. Moreover, he would have to handle the cash alone without taking anyone into confidence.

'Sir, I do understand the urgency of the matter, but this is indeed a very unusual request,' Malhotra said, unable to conceal the slight hesitation in his tone despite his best effort.

'Alright, Mr. Malhotra, why don't you then talk to PM Madam herself?'

Malhotra sat up straight again, and before he could tell Haksar that there was no need to bother the Prime Minister, the familiar voice of Indira Gandhi was heard at the other end. 'Hello, this is the Prime Minister speaking.'

'Hello, Madam...' said Malhotra, desperately searching for words. Before he had the chance to convey his regards and mention how honoured he felt to be entrusted with a task of national significance, the Prime Minister cut him short. 'My secretary must have informed you that we need an amount of sixty lakh rupees to be immediately transferred to Bangladesh for a secret mission, and we need your help. I request you to kindly prioritise this. Please get the money ready, and hand it over personally to our courier at the location mentioned by Mr. Haksar. I respect the fact that you are an honest and responsible employee of the bank, and I promise that we will take care of formalities immediately after the handover.'

The assurance from the Prime Minister was enough to soothe Malhotra's frayed nerves. He had one last question. He asked the Prime Minister, 'Madam, how would I recognise the courier?'

'I thought Mr. Haksar had mentioned it,' pat came the reply. 'We will be using code words. The courier will introduce himself by saying "I am Bangladesh *ka Babu*". In response, you should say "I am Bar-at-Law". Once you have handed the money over to him, you may come down to my house by 1 p.m., and collect the receipt. Please get down to business without further delay.'

As the line went dead, Malhotra took a deep breath and leaned back in his chair with his eyes closed, reflecting for a few seconds on the conversation he had just had with none other than the Prime Minister of the country! He had spent his entire life in a secure, albeit mundane job, with the sole purpose of earning his daily bread, and now, destiny had suddenly offered him a rare opportunity to be of service to the nation in a mission that apparently was of geopolitical significance. It was, undoubtedly, a once-in-a-lifetime opportunity, and he had better get about the job without losing any time.

***

Malhotra went to the deputy Chief Cashier, Ram Prakash Batra.

'How many bundles of hundreds do you have?' he asked.

Batra checked the cash register and replied, 'About a hundred and eighty to a hundred and ninety bundles, Sir.'

Malhotra mentally calculated that the money that Batra had would add up to less than two lakhs. They needed to get more money from the strongroom.

'Batra,' Malhotra said, 'we urgently need sixty lakhs in cash. Get the money from the strongroom, and load the bundles into a chest. We do not have much time.'

Batra was surprised at the sudden requirement for so much money in cash but did not ask questions. He went to the cabin of the cash-in-charge, Hakumat Rai Khanna, and told him about Malhotra's urgent request for sixty lakh rupees in cash. The two of them were the joint custodians of the keys to the strongroom. Before long,

Malhotra joined the two, and Khanna asked him why he needed so much money from the strongroom. Malhotra replied, 'The money is for a confidential mission. I cannot talk about it now. I will explain everything once the disbursement is completed.'

Without further ado, Batra and Khanna headed towards the strongroom. They entered the strongroom and started loading a chest with wads of hundred-rupee notes. Malhotra also walked into the strongroom to supervise them. Once the entire amount of sixty lakh rupees had been loaded into the chest, two porters were summoned.

Malhotra went back to his cabin and called up the security office, requesting an Ambassador car for himself, explaining that he had to leave the bank urgently on a confidential mission. He added that he would be driving the car himself and would not need the services of a chauffeur. Malhotra was told that, as per the policy of the bank, he would be provided with a car but would not be allowed to drive it himself. In fact, he would not be provided with the car keys either.

In the meantime, Batra and Khanna had locked the strongroom, and Batra had met the head cashier, Rawail Singh, to record the withdrawal of sixty lakh rupees in the vault register.

Malhotra came down to the gate of the bank premises, where the car allotted to him was waiting, with the driver and a security guard standing next to it. The two porters carried the chest to the car. The chest, however, did not fit inside the boot, which remained open.

Malhotra walked up to the driver, and before the latter could react, Malhotra snatched the car keys from him, got into the car and drove off. He had just started driving when he remembered that he was to visit the Prime Minister's residence to collect the receipt after handing the money over to the courier; hence, he might be delayed. He immediately turned around and drove back to the bank. He informed his deputy, Batra, to take care of business till he was back. He then drove off again.

Malhotra cast a quick glance at his watch. He was to meet the courier at half past twelve near Free Church. He had about fifteen minutes, and thankfully, his destination was not more than a hundred paces away from the bank.

***

Having reached the spot, Malhotra got out of the car and looked around. Soon, a tall, heavily built, fair-skinned man, wearing an olive-green cap, walked across the road and approached Malhotra. When he was about an arm's length away, the man said, 'I am Bangladesh *ka Babu*.'

Malhotra realised that he had met the right person. 'I am Bar-at-Law,' he said, just as the Honourable Prime Minister had instructed him.

The man looked at the car that Malhotra had been driving and said in a tone of urgency, 'Let us go!'

Malhotra was a bit surprised. He had no idea that he would have to drive the man to his destination as well. Getting behind the wheel, Malhotra asked the man, 'Where are we headed?'

'It would be helpful if you could drop me near Palam Airport,' said the man.

Malhotra started driving immediately. 'The chest is heavy,' he said, with a slight tilt of his head in the direction of the boot. 'I will accompany you to the airport.'

The man thought for a few seconds and said, 'That may not look proper. After all, I am on a confidential government mission and will be boarding an Air Force plane. I should rather hire a taxi and proceed. Why don't you drop me near a taxi stand?' He looked at his watch and said, 'I believe you are in a hurry, too. You should be visiting the Prime Minister now to collect the receipt.'

Malhotra nodded and stopped the car at a taxi stand near the crossing of Panchsheel Marg. The man got off the car and hailed a Fiat taxi.

The driver was a turbaned Sikh. Malhotra requested the driver to help them move the chest. The driver agreed readily, and the three men moved the chest from the boot of the Ambassador to that of the Fiat, which remained open as well.

Malhotra made a note of the registration number of the taxi and handed over the key of the chest to the courier. The latter thanked Malhotra profusely with folded hands. 'My name is Aziz,' the man said. 'Jai Bangladesh! Jai Bharat Mata!'

As Malhotra stood in the middle of the thoroughfare on that busy Monday afternoon, his eyes were moist with the realisation that he had contributed to the grand history of the two neighbouring nations in his limited capacity, and he would cherish that moment for the rest of his life. 'Jai Bangladesh! Jai Bharat Mata!' He echoed the man, his voice choking, and after a brief pause, said, 'Sir, I must now rush to the Prime Minister's house.'

The man gestured at the taxi driver to start driving.

Malhotra did not know that the man who sped off in the taxi with sixty lakh rupees was Rustom Sohrab Nagarwala, a former Captain in the Indian Army, who had just now pulled off one of the biggest and most mysterious money heists in the history of India.

***

Rustom Sohrab Nagarwala, forty-nine years old at the time of the heist, was born on March 2, 1922, in Bombay.

Goolbai, Nagarwala's mother, after losing her husband within four and a half years of their marriage, began to stay with her brother and later, left Bombay with her son, Rustom, whom she fondly called Russi, and her daughter, Armaity, to settle down in Pune. With limited means, Goolbai struggled to bring up her children.

Nagarwala went to school in Pune. After completing his Intermediate of Arts studies, he joined the Indian Army as an officer and was with the Army Ordnance Cops from 1943 to 1951.

An incident in 1947 bears testimony to the fact that Nagarwala had always been up for easy money, often throwing caution and integrity to the winds. In 1947, Nagarwala was posted in Punjab during Partition. In the same year, when he visited his mother in Pune, he requested one of her neighbours to lend him a sum of twenty-five thousand rupees for what he claimed were some unforeseen, critical expenses. Nagarwala convinced the gullible gentleman that he had buried in the compound of the officers' mess in Ambala, a substantial amount of money, which he, along with another officer, had collected from refugees whom they had helped cross the border. He had not been able to dig the cash out yet, as the other officer had his eyes on the booty. As soon as he managed to recover the money, he would pay double the money back to the gentleman. The latter believed Nagarwala and lent him the money. He never got his money back.

In 1949, during his leave, Nagarwala met with a life-changing accident when his motorbike collided with two stationary lorries, which did not have their parking lights turned on. He sustained grievous injuries and was under critical care for four days. As he started healing after suffering for months, he met with another accident and got the same leg broken. He spent two years in different hospitals, where he underwent multiple surgeries. His leg was saved, but he developed a limp and would constantly be in pain. Just as he had anticipated, Nagarwala was discharged from the army in 1951. Without any formal qualification or special skill, he was jobless. He visited Delhi several times and met government officials, requesting compensation and pension for his services in the army, finally having to settle for a paltry monthly pension of thirty-five rupees.

Nagarwala invested ten thousand rupees from his savings in Marina Taxi Service, a transport company in Delhi, which had been started by his friend, Rajinder Singh. He began to earn about five hundred rupees a month from the company.

Around this time, Nagarwala was often seen in the company of a woman, Jeanette Spears, who worked as a personal secretary in the US

Embassy in New Delhi. They had been introduced to each other by a common friend. Although it was evident that the two of them were very much in love, they could not get married, as Jeanette would lose her job in the Embassy if she did. Jeanette was soon posted to Japan.

With limited earnings in India, Nagarwala was finding it difficult to make two ends meet. He decided to travel to Japan to be with his 'American girlfriend'. In Japan, they lived in Nagoya. There, Nagarwala taught English at the American Culture Center and at the University of Nagoya.

Foreigners were required to leave Japan periodically and apply for a fresh visa every time to enter the country again. Nagarwala used the rule to his advantage. He would bring watches, tape recorders, and cameras from Japan and sell them at higher prices in India. Likewise, he carried back with him Indian jewellery and other items that would be of interest in Japan and sold them there at premium prices. Even after Jeanette had been transferred to Oslo, Nagarwala stayed back in Japan and carried on with his 'business'. He had to stop when he ran into problems with the customs authorities in India during one of his visits. Thereafter, he could not afford to go back to Japan.

The next few years were eventful. Nagarwala met with a car accident on his way to Pune from Bombay, in which his skull was fractured and his jaw and several teeth were broken. He also sustained injuries in the upper part of his body. He visited Ceylon (now, Sri Lanka) to meet Jeanette who had been posted there and who had visited Nagarwala when he had met with the car accident. He bought a burial plot next to Jeanette's in the US. He lived an idyllic life in

Pune, where he would wake up late, go out after lunch, and spend his evenings playing cards in the Gymkhana Club. He indulged in his love for horse racing and got into a habit of borrowing money from his friends or asking them to clear his debts instead of working hard. In the process, he also lost some friends.

Later, he shifted to Delhi and worked there as a tourist guide and a driver in the taxi services company he had set up with Rajinder Singh. He also taught English to a few Japanese students in Delhi and tried his luck in high-stake bridge. In his initial days in the capital, he stayed as a paying guest with one of his friends but left the house and moved to the Parsi Dharamshala after an altercation with him. Most of the time, he did not have any money and lived in fear of being thrown out of the *dharamshala* if he failed to pay his rent.

Though Nagarwala was conversant in several languages, including English, Hindi, Marathi, Gujarati, French, and Japanese, and his friend, Pudumjee, who had served in the Indian Army with him, arranged for some letters of recommendation, he failed to find a job. He continued to live the life of a tramp, never shying away from crossing the boundaries of morality and integrity to make quick and easy money, till he found himself in front of Free Church on Parliament Street on that fateful day, which would change his life forever.

***

After Nagarwala had left, Malhotra drove fast through the busy afternoon traffic towards the Prime Minister's residence at 1, Safdarjung Road. The last thing he wanted was to miss the deadline of 1 p.m.

It was a quarter to one when Malhotra reached the reception of the official complex at 1, Akbar Road that led to the Prime Minister's residence. There, Malhotra met Inspector Balram, who was an old acquaintance.

After the exchange of pleasantries, Malhotra told Balram with a courteous smile, 'I would like to meet the Prime Minister.'

Balram's eyebrows rose. 'Why do you want to see the Prime Minister?' he asked Malhotra.

'It's the Prime Minister who wanted to meet me at her residence,' Malhotra said, without revealing any details of the secret mission.

Balram said, 'Well, I'm afraid she is not home. She is in the Parliament. As you may be aware, today is the first day of the Lok Sabha session.'

Malhotra checked his watch again. He had, indeed, reached the Prime Minister's residence on time. He wondered why the Prime Minister had asked him to visit her at 1 p.m. when she must have known that she would be in the Parliament at that time. He was lost in thought for a few seconds. Then, he said, 'Well, if the Prime Minister is not here, I would like to meet Mr. Haksar, her principal secretary.'

Balram was rather intrigued by Malhotra's requests. He wondered what the banker was up to, but he thought it better not to probe.

'As I told you, Malhotra, the Parliament is in session, and the Prime Minister is there along with her principal secretary,' Balram replied. Sensing his friend's disappointment, Balram added, 'I can offer a suggestion. The Prime Minister and her officials usually use Gate No. 5 of Parliament House. Why don't you go there and wait for her?'

Around this time, two cars arrived at the complex in quick succession. On both occasions, Malhotra, much to the chagrin of the security personnel, ran to the cars, hoping to find Mr. Haksar, but he was disappointed on both the occasions.

After a few minutes, he walked up to the reception desk and asked, 'Does anyone know when the Prime Minister would be back from the Parliament House?' He did not receive an answer and went back to his seat. After a few more minutes, he went to the reception desk once again and asked restlessly, 'Is it possible to call the Prime Minister and inform her that I am waiting at the reception desk at her residence to meet her?' This time, Malhotra was informed that the Prime Minister could not be called.

'When does she usually return to her residence?' Malhotra asked again, his patience beginning to wear off.

'She is usually back here by 1:30,' said the staff member manning the desk.

'Alright, when is Mr. Haksar expected to return?' Malhotra asked next.

'Why don't you visit the Prime Minister's Secretariat? You may find Haksar there when he returns from the Parliament House,' he was told. Malhotra liked the suggestion and raced back to his car. He drove to South Block where the secretariat was located.

At the secretariat, Malhotra was told that the principal secretary had left a while back. What if he had gone over to the Prime Minister's residence to meet Malhotra there? As the idea struck him, Malhotra went back to the Akbar Road office only to find that neither Haksar nor the Prime Minister had returned.

Next, Malhotra drove to the Parliament House and was informed that the Prime Minister had gone for lunch. Assuming that the Prime Minister had gone to her residence to have lunch, Malhotra drove back to Akbar Road again. There, he learnt that the Prime Minister's lunch had been sent to the Parliament House.

Malhotra returned to the Parliament House and wanted to meet the Prime Minister but was informed that she was taking lunch in a private room, where visitors were not allowed.

Malhotra felt exhausted, shuttling back and forth, even as he was running out of time. Out of sheer desperation, Malhotra decided to take advantage of his acquaintance with S. S. Chaddha, an officer of the rank of Deputy Superintendent of Police (DSP), who was then the Personal Security Officer of the Prime Minister.

'Inform S. S. Chaddha that his friend, Ved Prakash Malhotra, Chief Cashier at the Parliament Street branch of State Bank of India, would like to meet him,' Malhotra told the guard at the Parliament gate. He had barely finished speaking when he saw Chaddha walking out of the building. It seemed to Malhotra that his prayers had finally been answered. He ran to Chaddha. Without wasting time on pleasantries, he said, 'I need to meet either the Prime Minister or her principal secretary. The matter is urgent, and the PM herself wanted to meet me.'

'Wait, let me check if you can meet her now,' said Chaddha.

Leaving Malhotra at the gate, Chaddha went inside. He returned after a few minutes.

'You'll have to wait. The PM is in a meeting,' Chaddha told Malhotra.

'Please go in and speak to the PM yourself. Tell her that I have been trying to meet her since 1 p.m. I am sure she will find the time to meet me,' Malhotra said frantically.

Chaddha went back inside and after a while, returned with N. K. Seshan, the Prime Minister's private secretary. Seshan listened to Malhotra patiently. Then, he called up Haksar, who was then at the secretariat office in South Block, and asked him to come down to the Prime Minister's Office in the Parliament House at the earliest.

Haksar met Malhotra at Gate No. 5 of the Parliament House. When Malhotra finished narrating to Haksar the course of events since the morning, the latter was stunned. 'Mr. Malhotra, you should immediately go to the nearest police station and file a complaint. I believe this is a matter of "extraordinary fraud", because no one from the Prime Minister's Office made the call to which you are referring. Not me, not Madam Prime Minister,' said Haksar.

Malhotra could not believe what he had just heard. The colour drained from his face, and he broke into a sweat. 'I thought I was doing my patriotic duty…' he mumbled faintly.

Haksar patted Malhotra on the back, wondering if the man was in his right mind, and went inside the Parliament House to meet the Prime Minister. On being briefed about the events that had transpired, the Prime Minister also commented that there had been 'an extraordinary case of fraud'. Haksar wondered if someone had played a 'prank on the bank'.

Malhotra stood outside the Parliament House, tense and confused. He kept insisting on talking to the Prime Minister but was not allowed to do so. After some time, Malhotra saw the Prime Minister leaving the Parliament House. 'PM Ma'am!' he screamed in vain from a distance. 'I am Ved Prakash Malhotra, Chief Cashier at the Parliament Street branch of the SBI! We talked on the phone this morning about a secret mission. You wanted me to meet you at your residence at 1 p.m.!' The Prime Minister did not look back. As she got into her car and was driven off, it seemed as if the ground had slipped from beneath Malhotra's feet.

Malhotra met B. N. Mehra, SP with Delhi Police, who was an old acquaintance. Mehra listened to the fantastic course of events and advised Malhotra to immediately go to Vijay Chowk to meet Y. Rajpal, District SP. Rajpal was at Vijay Chowk to oversee the police arrangements for a demonstration of the Bharatiya Jana Sangh workers. Mehra also called a sub-inspector to accompany Malhotra.

On reaching Vijay Chowk, Malhotra could not find Rajpal. Instead, he met Devinder Kumar Kashyap, Assistant Superintendent of Police (ASP). Kashyap listened to Malhotra's account and immediately sent out instructions on the police wireless network to trace the taxi, driven by a turbaned Sikh driver, in which the courier had escaped. Malhotra had noted down the number of the taxi, which was also shared on the wireless network. Kashyap wanted the taxi to be brought down to the Parliament Street Police Station, along with the driver.

Malhotra and Kashyap, accompanied by an Inspector by the name of Hari Dev, then went to the Parliament Street Police Station and met the district head, Rajpal. Rajpal listened to Malhotra's account and asked the officers to visit the Parliament Street branch of State Bank of India and validate the facts. The officers left immediately, leaving Malhotra with Rajpal. Rajpal and Malhotra were shortly joined by Inspector A. K. Bose, the Station House Officer (SHO) of the Tughlaq Road Police Station, who had been summoned by Kashyap.

In the bank, Kashyap and Hari Dev found out that Malhotra had indeed got an amount of sixty lakhs withdrawn from the strongroom in currency notes of hundred rupees and had left with the money in a car provided by the bank. Kashyap also checked the vault register, which showed an entry for the cash withdrawal. He then seized the register. S. K. Taparia, then Deputy Secretary of State Bank of India, had received a call from N. K. Seshan, Private Secretary to the Prime Minister, checking if an amount of sixty lakhs had indeed been withdrawn from the bank, as Malhotra had told Seshan. Taparia had confirmed to Seshan that Malhotra's account was correct. After the completion of the preliminary investigation at the bank, Kashyap, along with Hari Dev, S. K. Taparia, and Rawail Singh, Head Cashier, headed back to the Parliament Street Police Station, where Malhotra was being interrogated.

Rajpal, in the meantime, had received a call from the Prime Minister's Office (PMO) and had been informed that the case would be handled by the Crime Branch. Rajpal wanted the district officers to join hands with the Crime Branch to solve the case. He ordered Kashyap to lead the investigation on behalf of the district, assisted by Inspector Hari Dev and Inspector A. K. Bose.

A few hours later, Kashyap received a message that the taxi had been found at Shanti Path. Kashyap immediately left, along with Hari Dev.

***

It was around 3:30 pm in the afternoon when the middle-aged Sikh driver, Balbir Singh, was located by the police at Shanti Path. The taxi had broken down, and the driver was getting it repaired. In no time, at least five police jeeps arrived at the spot and surrounded the driver. Balbir was taken aback at the suddenness of the developments. He heard an instruction on one of the wireless sets that his taxi should immediately be brought down to the Parliament Street Police Station. On being informed that the taxi had broken down and could not be taken to the police station at that moment, the speaker on the wireless set ordered that Balbir Singh should be brought down right away.

When Balbir Singh arrived in a police jeep at the Parliament Street Police Station, he was identified by Malhotra as the one who had driven off with the mysterious courier after Malhotra had dropped him near the crossing of Panchsheel Marg. Likewise, Balbir recognised Malhotra and said that he, indeed, was the man who had got down from a black Ambassador and hailed his taxi at the Panchsheel crossing.

'They had a big chest in the boot of the Ambassador. I helped them load it in the boot of my taxi,' Balbir said.

'Did you manage to hear anything that the two men discussed between themselves?' asked Hari Dev.

Balbir thought for a few seconds and said, 'I remember them saying "Jai Bangladesh! Jai Bharat Mata!". He then pointed at Malhotra and added, 'What also struck me was this gentleman here saying that he had to rush immediately to the house of the Prime Minister! I thought the two must be very important persons.'

'What happened next?'

'I drove towards Palam as I had been told to,' Balbir continued. 'When we reached the Air Force area, the man asked me if we could reach the Air Force aerodrome in the next five to six minutes. When I informed him that it would take at least twenty minutes, the man shook his head and said that he would take the next flight in that case. He asked me to turn towards Ring Road. I followed his instructions. When we reached Defence Colony, he gave me directions to a bungalow, A-196. The Government Higher Secondary School was opposite to the bungalow. The man got off the taxi, and the two of us unloaded the chest from the boot. The man paid me the fare, and I drove off towards the Lodhi Colony taxi stand.'

'Was there anyone on the road who can tell us what happened after you had dropped the man off?'

'There was another taxi on the road, Sir,' Balbir said. 'It was a Fiat car, with one of the rear tyres punctured. I know that taxi and its driver, Dhian Singh. He is from the Lodhi Colony taxi stand.'

The police went to the Lodhi Colony taxi stand immediately and found the taxi. Dhian Singh told the police that he had, indeed, seen a tall and fair-complexioned man get off a taxi in Defence Colony. The man was wearing a cap, and he lit a cigarette after he had got a chest off the boot of the taxi with the help of the driver, Balbir Singh. After some time, the man hailed another taxi on the same road, loaded his chest in the boot of the taxi with the help of its driver, and was driven off.

'The reasons why I remember the incident are the huge chest that was unloaded from the boot of the taxi and the behaviour of the man, which I found rather strange. He was wearing an olive-coloured cap, which he took off and threw into the drain! He looked restless,' said Dhian Singh.

'Do you, by any chance, know the taxi driver who drove him from Defence Colony?' Hari Dev asked.

'I do,' said Dhian Singh. 'I have seen him drive students from Jorbagh to and from the school in Defence Colony.'

The police went to the Government Higher Secondary School and spoke to some of the students. They gathered details of when and where the taxi would arrive to pick up the students. The police headed for the specified location, accompanied by Dhian Singh, who had seen the driver. When the taxi was located, Dhian Singh identified its driver, the fifty-five-year-old Om Prakash.

Om Prakash then narrated to the police the bizarre sequence of events that unfolded after he had picked up the mysterious passenger with the big steel chest in 'A' Block of Defence Colony that afternoon.

***

'That chest in the boot is very heavy. Are there books in it?' Om Prakash asked, looking at his passenger in the rear view mirror.

'Yes, there are books in it,' Nagarwala replied curtly. His mind was working overtime, trying to figure out the next course of action.

'Well, you will need to pay extra,' Om Prakash said.

'That's fine,' Nagarwala readily agreed, adding, 'let us go to Delhi Gate.'

As the taxi approached the Parsi Dharamshala on Bahadur Shah Zafar Marg, Nagarwala asked Om Prakash to stop. He had realised that he needed to get rid of the bank chest at the earliest. He needed bags into which he could load the wads of hundred-rupee notes. Once the taxi had come to a halt, he stepped out and went inside. He returned after about fifteen minutes, carrying an empty bag.

Getting inside the taxi, Nagarwala instructed Om Prakash to drive him to Rajinder Nagar. Nagarwala had figured out that the area would be deserted at that time of the day and would be the ideal place for emptying the chest. However, the driver had to be taken into confidence.

On the way, Nagarwala started making small talk with Om Prakash, asking him questions about where he was from, his family, where he lived in Delhi, and how much he earned every day. As the car approached Rajinder Nagar, Nagarwala said, 'Now that we know each other well, I will share a secret with you. You must promise me that you will keep the secret to yourself.'

Om Prakash nodded, looking into the rear view mirror, his brows wrinkled.

Nagarwala said, 'The chest in the boot doesn't contain books.'

Om Prakash listened with bated breath.

Nagarwala said, 'The chest contains sixty lakh rupees.' After a brief pause, he added, 'I will have to transfer the money from the chest to the bag.'

Om Prakash could not believe his ears. He had never in his entire life seen or even heard of so much money. It felt surreal to think that all that money was in the boot of his taxi at that very moment! He gulped and said, '*Saab*, you seem to be a very rich man! Why would you handle so much cash inside a taxi on the open road? You should transfer the money from the chest in a more private place, in my opinion.'

Nagarwala said, 'You are right. But, you see, I must take the money to Bangladesh immediately. I cannot carry the chest around, looking for a private place, as I am running out of time.'

Om Prakash nodded. He drove as per Nagarwala's instructions, and when the car reached a park in a deserted area, he was asked to stop the car.

'Stay inside,' Nagarwala said, as he got off the car.

Om Prakash turned around to keep an eye on his passenger, and what he saw took his breath away. The man was carrying a revolver! It was inside a holster, tucked at his waist and covered by his shirt.

Nagarwala looked at the chest inside the open boot and realised that one bag would not be sufficient to hold all the money. He had a friend in 'R' Block, who might be able to help him. He got into the taxi and asked Om Prakash to drive further ahead. After he had driven a few metres, Om Prakash was asked to stop near 'R' Block. Nagarwala got off the car and walked towards a nearby house. He called out to someone, and a man appeared on the first floor. The two spoke in English, unintelligible to Om Prakash, and shortly afterwards, Nagarwala stepped into the house. After a while, he returned with a Rexine bag.

As ordered by his passenger, Om Prakash started driving again. When the taxi reached a desolate area at the end of 'R' Block, Nagarwala asked Om Prakash to stop. Om Prakash looked around. A jungle on one side, a few houses far between on the other side, not a soul around, a strange man in the taxi with a revolver, and a chest in the boot with sixty lakh rupees—the situation could not get any more dangerous. His heart thudded against his ribs. He was becoming increasingly suspicious of the activities of his passenger.

Nagarwala asked Om Prakash once again to remain inside and stepped out of the taxi. This time, he opened the boot and began to transfer bundles of cash from the chest into the bags he had been carrying. Once the chest had been emptied, Nagarwala pulled it out of the boot and dropped it by the side of the road near a dustbin. He placed the loaded bags inside the taxi and got into it.

Om Prakash was sweating profusely, and his throat and mouth were dry. He looked into the rear view mirror and said, '*Saab*, I request you to take another taxi.'

Nagarwala laughed out loud. 'You are scared, are you? I don't blame you. You've never seen so much money in all your life, I believe. Even your forefathers must not have, I am sure. Don't worry. I am not a robber. This money is for a mission in Bangladesh. Remember this: by helping me, you are serving a national cause.' After thinking for a few seconds, he added, 'Alright, drop me off at Connaught Place.'

On reaching Connaught Place, Nagarwala got off in front of a furniture shop near Marina Hotel. Before leaving, he offered Om Prakash five hundred rupees. When the driver politely declined, Nagarwala left five one-hundred-rupee notes in the back seat of the taxi and left.

Om Prakash then drove off.

Nagarwala thought that leaving the taxi was a good idea. Since the idiot knew his secret, was scared, and would also not accept cash, it was better that he had no further knowledge about Nagarwala's movements. Nagarwala also realised that it was not safe to walk along the streets of Delhi in broad daylight with two bags loaded with currency notes worth sixty lakhs. He had to leave the bags somewhere safe from where they could be retrieved at an opportune time.

***

Nagarwala got a shave and got his hair cut short and dyed. Then, he walked into the Marina Hotel, carrying the two bags. He spoke to the concierge and sought his permission to leave the bags in the patio of the hotel under his watchful eyes for some time, promising that he would be back shortly.

Next, Nagarwala went to the office of Marina Taxi Service. This was the same company that had been started by his friend, Rajinder Singh, and in which he had invested ten thousand rupees about two decades ago. Rajinder's son, Mohinder, was now in charge of the business.

Mohinder was not in office. Nagarwala waited till about a quarter to three when Mohinder returned. Nagarwala told him that he would need an air-conditioned car to take a few guests, all of them foreign nationals, on a trip to Nainital and Ranikhet. Mohinder respected Nagarwala deeply, because the later had not only invested in the business two decades back but also was a loyal customer, was prompt with clearing his dues, and was loved by the drivers for his generous tips. However, on that particular day, there was no car available. Nagarwala then requested Mohinder to send an air-conditioned car to the Parsi Dharamshala the next day, as early in the morning as possible. Mohinder made a booking in the name of Nagarwala and confirmed that the car would be at his disposal the next morning.

Nagarwala then asked Mohinder if he could use the latter's own car for a few hours to take care of a few personal errands and to meet his guests. Mohinder readily agreed and summoned his private chauffeur, Paramjit. Handing the car keys to Paramjit, Mohinder instructed him not to ask Nagarwala for money and to return as soon as Nagarwala released him from duty.

Nagarwala asked Mohinder where he could buy a big leather suitcase. Mohinder mentioned a couple of shops in the vicinity. Harbhajan, Mohinder's brother, offered to accompany Nagarwala to Imperial Leather Works, which was a prominent seller of leather goods in Delhi.

Nagarwala bought two leather suitcases from the store. As Harbhajan waited in the office of Marina Taxi Service with the suitcases, Nagarwala went back to Marina Hotel. He thanked the concierge profusely for allowing him to keep the two bags in the patio of the hotel, picked up the bags, and returned to the office of Marina Taxi Service. With the help of Paramjit, Nagarwala loaded the bags in the boot of Mohinder's private car.

'Take me to the Parsi Dharamshala,' Nagarwala told Paramjit, as he got into the car. He needed to transfer the cash to the suitcases.

Nagarwala reached his destination in less than ten minutes. The two men unloaded all the bags—two empty leather suitcases and two bags containing the money. Nagarwala then went straight to his room, barely taking notice of Dhur Darius Bagli, the wife of the priest-caretaker of the *dharamshala*, who was surprised by Nagarwala's uncharacteristic absentmindedness and also by the fact that Nagarwala's hair was short and dyed. Nagarwala had been staying in Room No. 3, a double occupancy room, since November 1970 and was cordial with everyone.

After about fifteen minutes, Nagarwala came out of the *dharamshala* and returned to the car. Nagarwala requested Paramjit to help him carry the two leather suitcases from his room to the car, and Paramjit complied.

Nagarwala now had to leave the suitcases with someone he could trust and who would not ask too many uncomfortable questions. He asked Paramjit to drive him to Kashmere Gate. However, when the car reached Nicholson Road, Nagarwala stepped out of the car in front of a two-storey house. Nagarwala opened the boot and pulled out one of the suitcases. Asking Paramjit to wait in the car, Nagarwala went inside the house, which belonged to Lt. Col. P. S. Keshwala. Nagarwala put the suitcase down on the staircase and sprinted to the flat.

When Nagarwala rang the bell, the door was opened by Keshwala's wife. 'Please come in, *bhai saab*. Your friend is not at home. He could be at the British Council Library or at Mrs. Badhwar's place,' she said. 'Please make yourself comfortable. Will you have some tea?'

Nagarwala declined the offer of tea. He asked casually, 'Would you mind if your husband and I go out of town for a few days?' Taking his friend along on a vacation would look perfectly natural and would be a legitimate excuse for keeping his valuables in a suitcase in that house, instead of leaving them at the *dharamshala*.

Mrs. Keshwala was mildly surprised. 'Oh, why would I mind? You should ask your friend,' she said.

'Of course, I will,' said Nagarwala. 'I will leave a suitcase here while we are away on our trip. I hope it won't be too much trouble,' he added.

Mrs. Keshwala looked hesitant. The man had been acting weird. What was he up to? Without waiting for the lady's reply, Nagarwala stepped out and returned promptly, carrying the suitcase he had left in the staircase. Paramjit kept watching the strange actions of his passenger and was intrigued.

When Mrs. Keshwala saw the suitcase, she said, 'I'm sorry, *bhai saab*, but we don't have enough space for a suitcase so big!'

Nagarwala did not insist. He picked up the suitcase and went back to the car, looking visibly angry. He took a while to catch his breath and then wiped the sweat off his face with a handkerchief. The afternoon heat was making him feel sick and irritable. He asked Paramjit to take him back to Connaught Place, hoping that he would be able to find his friend, Lt Col Keshwala, at the residence of Mohini Badhwar, as Mrs. Keshwala had suggested. Maybe his friend would be of help, even if the wife had turned him away.

Mrs. Badhwar was a common friend of Nagarwala and Lt Col Keshwala. Nagarwala did find his friend there, although the hostess herself was not around. With his bets still on his plan, Nagarwala offered to take his friend along on a trip to Ranikhet, even enticing him with the prospect of making some quick money from the trip. When Lt Col Keshwala refused to accompany him on any such trip, even questioning the legitimacy of the proposed earning, Nagarwala realised that he would need to make an alternate plan to dispose of the suitcases.

Nagarwala asked the lieutenant colonel if he could use the latter's private car for a few hours. Nagarwala decided that he would drive the car himself, as he did not want anyone to know where he had kept the suitcases. Lt Col Keshwala's car was being used at the time by Mrs. Badhwar. Nagarwala called her up, requested her to send the car across, and promised that he would return the car by the evening.

When the car arrived, Nagarwala got the suitcases shifted to its boot with the help of Paramjit, who had, in the meantime, been getting increasingly annoyed with the random movements of the man across the city and the handling of those heavy suitcases. There definitely was something fishy about him! When Paramjit was finally paid for his services and asked to leave, he heaved a sigh of relief. He promptly started on his way back to Mohinder's office in Connaught Place.

Nagarwala got into the driver's seat himself, promising his friend that he would return the car by seven in the evening. He had devised a new plan.

Nagarwala drove back to Defence Colony. His friend, Nashir B. Captain, stayed with his wife, Nergiz, in a *barsati* there. Captain had, in the past, stayed at the Parsi Dharamshala as Nagarwala's roommate when he had been transferred by *The Statesman*'s Kolkata office to New Delhi, before he had moved to the *barsati* in Defence Colony.

Daylight was beginning to fade when Nagarwala arrived at the residence of the Captain family. Nergiz had returned from her office at the British Council Library a while ago. When she opened the door on hearing the bell, she saw Nagarwala, looking dishevelled and exhausted, carrying two large suitcases. She invited him inside the house. Nagarwala said he would wait for his friend.

Captain reached home after some time. On seeing his friend, Nagarwala told him that he had come to return the money he had earlier borrowed from him. He gave him two envelopes—one contained eleven hundred rupees, the amount he owed to Captain after he had paid nine hundred out of the two thousand rupees he had borrowed, and the other had an amount of fifteen hundred rupees, which Nagarwala said he would collect after his return from Ranikhet.

Nagarwala then requested the Captain couple to keep the two suitcases, which, he said, belonged to a friend in the Parsi Dharamshala. The friend, Nagarwala said, was going to travel out of town and did not consider it safe to leave the bags at the *dharamshala*. The Captain couple had no reason to doubt Nagarwala and agreed to keep the suitcases. Nagarwala helped his friend move the suitcases under the bed.

It was around half past eight when Nagarwala reached Mrs. Badhwar's house and returned the car. Mrs. Badhwar, to her surprise, saw Nagarwala carrying a scooter tyre in his hand. He looked exhausted and had grease on his shirt. 'My scooter broke down,' Nagarwala told her sheepishly and left promptly, without bothering to stop for the tea he was offered.

***

Earlier in the day, based on the statements of Balbir Singh, Dhian Singh, and Om Prakash, the police went to Defence Colony. They thoroughly searched the neighbourhood of the bungalow, A-196, where Balbir Singh had dropped Nagarwala. The olive-green cap that Nagarwala had got rid of was, indeed, found in a drain, just as Dhian Singh had narrated. The police then went to the house in 'R' Block of New Rajinder Nagar, which Om Prakash had mentioned. They found that the house belonged to Homi C. Gotla. Nagarwala had befriended Gotla when the latter shared a room with him in the Parsi Dharamshala, before moving to his Rajinder Nagar residence.

'Did you have a visitor earlier in the afternoon who arrived here by a taxi?' Gotla was asked.

'Oh yes, that was my friend, Rustom Sohrab Nagarwala,' Gotla replied. 'Is everything alright?'

'Did you give him a Rexine bag?'

'Yes, my wife did.'

'Where does your friend stay?'

'He stays in the Parsi Anjuman Dharamshala on Bahadur Shah Zafar Marg,' Gotla replied. After a pause, he repeated, 'Is everything alright?'

'Your friend has committed a heinous crime,' the reply shocked Gotla. 'We will leave a few officers in plain clothes here to keep an eye on your house, in case your friend decides to pay you a visit again.'

Om Prakash took the police to the Marina taxi stand where he had dropped Nagarwala. The police started making inquiries in the area and eventually reached the office of Marina Taxi Service. Mohinder was in his office.

'Has anyone hired a car for an outstation journey today?' the police asked Mohinder. By that time, Mohinder had smelt a rat. It was not the first time that the police had turned up in the area. Earlier in the day, Inspector A. K. Bose and his team had been talking to drivers and taxi companies in the neighbourhood.

'A man by the name of Rustom Sohrab Nagarwala made a booking for a big, air-conditioned car for Nainital and Ranikhet earlier today,' said Mohinder, handing the booking register over to the police. 'One of my drivers has been taking him around the city,' he added, pointing at Paramjit, who had returned to the office by that time.

Paramjit told the police everything about Nagarwala's movements through the afternoon.

***

The quiet of the evening in the premises of the Parsi Dharamshala was shattered by the arrival of two police jeeps that stopped near the compound. Almost a dozen policemen, including ASP Kashyap, Inspector Hari Dev, and Inspector A. K. Bose, alighted from the jeeps. The three stormed into the *dharamshala* premises while the others took positions outside. On seeing the policemen, Dhur, the wife of the manager of the *dharamshala*, was startled, but she firmly asked the men in uniform why they had barged into the premises that housed a temple for Parsi Zoroastrians. The three men paid no heed and asked for the manager, Bagli. When Bagli appeared before the policemen, he was asked to lead the team to Room No. 3.

The room was not locked, and the policemen entered without any difficulty. They started going through the belongings of both occupants, none of whom was present in the room. The police also rummaged through their bags, which were not locked. Bagli tried to protest by asking if the police had a search warrant but was quickly silenced. He was told that a warrant was not mandatory in certain exceptional circumstances.

In no time, the room was turned upside down. The police found a revolver wrapped in a white shirt. Books, papers, and items of clothing were scattered everywhere. Going through the available documents, the police formed a fair idea about Nagarwala's profile—his early years in Pune, his service in the Indian Army, his stay in Japan where he had applied for a trade licence that had been rejected, his business connections in foreign countries like Sri Lanka, Hong Kong, and Japan, and his running a tourist taxi service, as well as working as a travel guide and driver in Delhi.

Around half past seven, a call was received at the *dharamshala*. Inspector Bose received the call. It was from a woman who claimed to be a friend of Nagarwala. When she was informed that Nagarwala was not in the *dharamshala*, she mentioned that it was Nagarwala who had asked her to call at that time. When Bose asked for her name and address, she disconnected the line.

The search having yielded a lot of information about Nagarwala, ASP Kashyap and Inspectors Hari Dev and A. K. Bose left for some much-needed rest. They left a team of policemen, along with the two taxi drivers, Balbir Singh and Om Prakash, at the *dharamshala*, in case Nagarwala returned during the night. The team was given Nagarwala's photographs, which the police had seized from his room. The manager and his wife were instructed to call the police as soon as Nagarwala returned.

***

It was around eight in the night when an auto rickshaw stopped outside the Parsi Dharamshala. Balbir Singh saw a man alight and walk into the *dharamshala*, carrying a scooter tyre and a Rexine bag. However, in the few seconds he had, he could not recognise Nagarwala, who had cut his hair short. Likewise, the policemen who had been given Nagarwala's photographs could not recognise him.

However, Mrs. Bagli recognised Nagarwala immediately. She ran into her room, her husband already inside. They called the police.

A couple of ladies who had been sitting with Mrs. Bagli rushed to the policemen positioned at the gate and informed them about Nagarwala's arrival.

In the meantime, Nagarwala had gone into his room. He was shocked to see the state it was in. He immediately headed towards Bagli's room.

Hearing Nagarwala's voice outside, Bagli told his wife, 'I don't want to talk to him. Get rid of him somehow!'

When Mrs. Bagli opened the door, Nagarwala asked, 'Where is Mr. Bagli? I want to talk to him right now!'

Mrs. Bagli, who was upset over the events of the day, said, 'He is not home.'

'I want to know who went inside my room. Someone has rummaged through my belongings!' Nagarwala sounded furious.

Mrs. Bagli gritted her teeth. 'The police were here,' she said, looking into Nagarwala's eyes. 'They believe you have stolen sixty lakhs from a bank!'

Nagarwala's heart skipped a beat. How did the police reach the *dharamshala*? However, he was quick to regain his composure. He exclaimed, 'What nonsense! Why didn't your husband stop them? Did they have a warrant?'

As the argument continued, two policemen rushed into the room and overpowered Nagarwala, each grabbing an arm. A third policeman had entered the room in the meantime and trained his service revolver on Nagarwala.

'I will get all of you suspended! You will have to pay a heavy price for this!' Nagarwala kept shouting and trying to free himself, even as he was taken outside and made to sit in a chair, while the policemen waited for their seniors to arrive.

The two taxi drivers now took a close look at the prisoner and identified him immediately as the man they had driven across the city earlier in the day. The police found bundles of hundred-rupee notes, amounting to thirty thousand rupees, inside the tyre, which was promptly seized.

ASP Kashyap and Inspectors Hari Dev and A. K. Bose were at the Tughlaq Road Police Station when they got to know through a message on the wireless set that Nagarwala had been caught at the *dharamshala*. They immediately rushed to the spot.

When they reached the *dharamshala*, Kashyap, Hari Dev, and Bose arrested Nagarwala and brought him to the Parliament Street Police Station, along with Balbir Singh and Om Prakash. A few policemen were asked to stay back at the *dharamshala* and keep an eye on Nagarwala's room and the premises in general.

***

Ved Prakash Malhotra had been waiting at the Parliament Street Police Station, ruminating over the fantastic events of the day. He was heartbroken with the realisation that all the respect he had earned in the last twenty-six years of his service to the bank had been decimated in just a day, thanks to an evil conspiracy that had robbed the bank of sixty lakh rupees. Malhotra was a veteran in the bank. Known for his sincerity and honesty, Malhotra had risen through the ranks to reach the esteemed position he had been enjoying, till a few hours back.

He was shaken out of his reverie by a sudden racket in the police station. He looked up and saw Nagarwala being brought in by a bunch of policemen.

Malhotra stood up, shaking with anger, his eyes bloodshot, his tears overflowing. 'Don't let this man go!' he screamed. 'He got an innocent man involved in his disgusting plan! He also has an accomplice, a lady. She pretended to be the Prime Minister and spoke to me in the morning. You must also catch hold of her!'

The police were relieved that Malhotra's outburst had served to establish eyewitness identification of the accused, which is a prerequisite for any investigation. One of the policemen walked up to Malhotra and said, 'There is no lady involved. This man imitated the voices of both the Prime Minister and her principal secretary.'

Malhotra looked unbelievingly at Nagarwala.

Nagarwala folded his hands. 'I am sorry,' he said to Malhotra and then turned to one of the policemen, adding, 'this man is innocent.' The police took him away for interrogation. They still had to complete the arduous task of recovering the money.

Nagarwala kept telling Hari Dev and Bose that the thirty thousand rupees which the police had found inside the scooter tyre was his share of the booty. The rest of the money had been taken away by another person he did not know. Even as senior officials joined the interrogation, Nagarwala did not deviate from his initial statement. The investigators then came up with an idea. They suggested that Deputy

Inspector General (DIG) P. A. Rosha, who had not met Nagarwala yet, should meet him in plain clothes and pretend to be an official with State Bank of India, offering to strike a deal with Nagarwala.

Accordingly, SP Rajpal and DIG Rosha met Nagarwala, and DIG Rosha was introduced to Nagarwala as a senior officer with the bank. Rosha convinced Nagarwala that the bank would offer him a generous reward if he helped in the recovery of the rest of the loot. After a while, Nagarwala agreed. He changed his statement and said that he knew where the rest of the money was hidden. He offered to lead the police to the spot on the conditions that the policemen should be in plain clothes as he did not want to be seen in the company of the police, and the police would treat him amicably as he had a heart ailment. He also mentioned that his friends—Gotla, who had given him the Rexine bag, Keshwala, whom he had approached to look after the loot while he stayed away from Delhi for a few days, Bagli, who was the manager of the Parsi Dharamshala, Captain, in whose residence the cash was hidden, and the lady, whom he called his girlfriend, who had called the *dharamshala* earlier that evening as they had planned to go away to Ranikhet on a holiday the next morning—were innocent and should not be harassed by the police.

The police seized the car that Malhotra had used to bring the money to Nagarwala. Then, they accompanied Nagarwala to the residence of the Captains.

It was around ten in the night when the team reached the *barsati*. Four or five officers went inside while the others were stationed outside. The Captains had retired for the day and were woken up by the doorbell, followed by a few knocks on the door. Nagarwala introduced the policemen in plain clothes as his friends and said that he had come to fetch the suitcases he had earlier left there. Two policemen entered the bedroom and pulled out the two suitcases from under the bed. As the team was leaving, Nagarwala told the Captains, 'I'll meet you as soon as I am back from Ranikhet.'

At the top of the stairs, one of the suitcases was opened by the police, and the wads of currency notes inside were checked to their satisfaction. As Nagarwala got into the police car, he saw his friend waving at him from the second floor, and he waved back.

The money was recovered.

***

Once the team was back at the Parliament Street Police Station, the suitcases were opened. When Malhotra was summoned to identify the cash, he confirmed that those, indeed, were the bundles of hundred-rupee notes that he had handed over to Nagarwala. As the police started counting the cash, Om Prakash, who had been given five one-hundred-rupee notes by Nagarwala earlier in the day, scornfully threw them into the suitcase.

In all, the police counted an amount of fifty-nine lakhs, ninety-four thousand and three hundred rupees in the two suitcases and the scooter tyre that had been seized earlier from Nagarwala. As such, there was a shortfall of five thousand and seven hundred rupees. Nagarwala told the police that he had returned an amount of twenty-six hundred rupees to his friend, Captain.

The suitcases were then sealed.

When Nagarwala saw DIG Rosha inside the station carrying out police duties, he realised that he had been fooled by the police.

***

The next morning, the news of the heist spread like wildfire. Press reporters and senior government officials visited the police stations as well as the Parliament Street branch of State Bank of India. In a late-night press conference, the police broke the seals on the suitcases and displayed the recovered cash to media persons. Nagarwala was also paraded before the press.

Kashyap continued the interrogation.

Nagarwala claimed that he had modulated his voice and spoken to Malhotra as both P. N. Haksar and Indira Gandhi from a telephone booth in the bank premises. He even mimicked the voice of Indira Gandhi a few times before the police to convince them. The police got him to speak in the voices of the Prime Minister and her principal secretary a few times on the telephone, in calls received by Malhotra, to check how he sounded over a telephone line. Kashyap was convinced and recorded his observation in the case diary.

Nagarwala talked about his service in the Indian Army, his accidents, and his visits to Japan to earn a livelihood. He mentioned that the heist had not been a pre-planned one, and that he had hit upon the idea when he had visited the bank in the morning to collect change for a one-hundred rupee note. 'I was posted in Ambala during Partition in 1947. The violence then had a traumatic effect on me, and what is happening now in Bangladesh is also unbearable. I wanted to do something sensational and draw everyone's attention to the cause of the freedom fighters in Bangladesh,' Nagarwala said in his statement. 'However, I regret what I have done. I have inadvertently damaged the career of an innocent and gullible man. I will confess to my crime in the court, but I am worried about the negative publicity in the media, which may ruin the rest of my life.'

***

Bose planned to visit Captain to recover the twenty-six hundred rupees, which Nagarwala had given him. Malhotra would be the key witness in the case, as it was his sharing of the number of Balbir Singh's taxi that eventually led to Nagarwala's arrest. As for the revolver that was found in Nagarwala's possession, he declared that it was a private revolver of 0.38 bore, for which he had not needed a separate licence while he had been in the army. However, after being discharged from the army, he had left for Japan in a rush for his treatment, and on his return to India, had not deposited the revolver with government authorities, unsure of the legal implications of his continued possession of the weapon for an extended period after leaving the armed forces.

The police decided that they would not press for Nagarwala's police remand, as he would confess to his crime in the court, and the money he had stolen had also been recovered. Nagarwala would be presented before a magistrate the next day. He was lodged in a cell at the Parliament Street Police Station, where he was provided with a salt-free diet and the medicines he took after he had suffered from a paralytic stroke. Balbir Singh and Om Prakash were asked to spend the night in a neighbouring cell to keep an eye on the accused.

In Bombay (now, Mumbai), seventy-five-year-old Goolbai heard on All India Radio the shocking news of her son's arrest as the sole perpetrator of a sixty- lakh rupees robbery in State Bank of India in Delhi. She was devastated and immediately destroyed the letters her son had written to her, fearing possible police action.

***

The next day, on May 25, the judicial magistrate in charge of the Parliament Street Police Station ordered a one-day judicial custody for Nagarwala, so that his confession could be recorded before a link magistrate, who is responsible for recording confessions and dying statements, conducting identification parades, and other functions. The judicial magistrate also approved the application moved by State Bank of India, seeking custody of the recovered cash. The police were instructed to hand the cash over to the bank, under the condition that the bank would present the seized cash as and when needed as part of the court proceedings.

Nagarwala was sent to Tihar Jail for a one-day judicial custody. Inquisitive prisoners rushed to meet the man who had mimicked the voice of Indira Gandhi to rob sixty lakh rupees from State Bank of India. Among them was Mohinder Kumar Shastri, a post-graduate in Sociology from Aligarh Muslim University, who was also conversant in legal matters. Shastri warned Nagarwala that if he confessed to the crime as he had planned, he might be convicted. Nagarwala, however, paid no heed to the warning. He was confident that if he confessed, he would be forgiven and released from jail.

The next day, on May 26, when Nagarwala was being taken to the court, he was accompanied by Shastri, among others, in the police van, as they were all scheduled to be produced in respective courts. All through the journey, Shastri kept trying to convince Nagarwala not to confess to his crime but in vain.

When Nagarwala was produced before the magistrate at around half past three, he was told that he was not bound by law to make a confessional statement and that his statement would be recorded only after ensuring that it was voluntary. However, if he did confess to his crime, it might be used against him as evidence. When Nagarwala insisted that his statement be recorded, the magistrate extended his judicial custody by another day to give him time to mull over his decision. Nagarwala accepted the extension, requesting that he be housed in a B-class jail that would ensure better facilities, considering that he was a former army serviceman and had physical disabilities.

The next day, on May 27, Nagarwala was produced again before the link magistrate. He was allowed an additional time of two hours, without any police intervention, to make sure that he was ready to record the confession of his own free will without any coercion. Nagarwala then made the confessional statement on camera.

Nagarwala said that he had acted on impulse. He wanted to do something sensational for the rebels in Bangladesh, and at the same time, come to the notice of the Prime Minister of India. The idea was entirely his own, and he did not have an accomplice. He regretted the fact that, acting on a whim, he had endangered the career of an honest man, Ved Prakash Malhotra, the Chief Cashier at the Parliament Street branch of State Bank of India. His own future was also at stake as he faced charges of fraud. However, he had never tried to escape. He had handed himself over to the police without any resistance. He had helped the police recover the cash. He had fully cooperated with the investigators and the judiciary. He had had an impeccable record of behaviour as a civilian as well as an officer in the army. In view of the above, he would expect the court to be lenient in dealing with him.

On May 24, 1971, Nagarwala happened to be in the vicinity of the Parliament Street branch of State Bank of India. He had gone inside the bank to collect change for a one-hundred-rupee note. Because of the scorching heat outside, he had stayed back inside the bank for a while. Suddenly, he had a brainwave. Looking around, he could see two phone booths near the bank. He walked past the counters inside the bank and reached the cabin of the Chief Cashier. Looking through the glass partition, he could see Malhotra speaking to a guest. Nagarwala stepped out of the bank, went to one of the phone booths, and looked up Malhotra's number from the directory listing.

Thereafter, Nagarwala narrated the incidents of the day, just as they had unravelled. However, it was detected later that the documented confession did not mention Nagarwala's meetings with Gotla, Lt. Col. Keshwala, Ms. Badhwar, and the Captain couple; the recovery of thirty thousand rupees from the tyre that Nagarwala had been carrying at the time of his arrest; Nagarwala's booking of an air-conditioned car for a trip to the hills the following day and the reason behind the planned visit; and the deal Nagarwala had made with the police—leading them to the money in exchange for his freedom.

The confessional statement was completed after about an hour. The link magistrate asked Nagarwala to go through the eight-page document and sign on every page if he approved of its contents. Once the formalities had been completed, the magistrate got the statement sealed and handed it over to his staff to be dispatched to the trial court.

In a last-minute decision, the place of occurrence of the crime was changed from the Parliament Street area to the Chanakya Puri area, since Malhotra had handed over the sixty lakh rupees to Nagarwala in the Chanakya Puri area. Nagarwala was produced before the magistrate in charge of the Chanakya Puri Police Station, and he pleaded guilty. The magistrate pronounced Nagarwala guilty under Sections 419 and 420 of the Indian Penal Code. Contrary to Nagarwala's expectations, the court sentenced him to four years of rigorous imprisonment and a fine of two thousand rupees.

Nagarwala's face did not betray any emotion. He was transported back to Tihar Jail.

The last-minute change in the location of occurrence of the crime and the speed of the trial evoked criticism in the media and the Opposition party of the time.

***

In the changed circumstances where Nagarwala was now a convict, he was deemed a C-class prisoner. He had been assigned to the carpentry section, where he had to make chairs. He was also getting increasingly annoyed with the curiosity of his fellow prisoners, who requested him repeatedly to mimic the voice of the Prime Minister. His friend, Shastri, had also been assigned to the carpentry section. Nagarwala was repentant and sought legal advice from Shastri.

Shastri suggested that Nagarwala should seek a retrial and appeal to the higher court. There were loopholes, such as the absence of two mandatory independent eyewitnesses signing the confession. However, Nagarkar did not have enough resources to fight a case. Shastri then advised Nagarwala to get in touch with Rajendra Kumar Maheshwari, a young lawyer from Delhi, who had, in the past, fought the case for a murder convict serving life imprisonment for free. The lawyer, in his pursuit of fame, might agree to take up Nagarwala's case. He visited the jail from time to time to meet his clients, and Shastri offered to set up a meeting. Surprisingly, Nagarwala did not heed the advice.

One day, as he waited outside the police van in front of the trial court, Nagarwala met his friend, Nusli Pudumjee. Pudumjee had been in Europe with his family when a common friend in Pune had shared with him details of the case. On his return to India, Pudumjee got in touch with a friend in Delhi, who arranged a meeting with Nagarwala, with the warning that the matter had taken on a political colour, and anyone who met Nagarwala ran the risk of coming under the scanner. But, Pudumjee was determined to help his friend, irrespective of potential consequences.

The meeting brought some cheer to Nagarwala, who had

been shunned by his friends ever since he had been convicted and imprisoned.

***

In the meantime, Maheshwari, determined to fight for Nagarwala, travelled across Pune and Bombay, meeting Nagarwala's friends and family, to gather information for his case. He met Nagarwala's mother, who pleaded with him to help her son. However, he faced difficulties eliciting information from Nagarwala himself.

On June 21, Maheshwari filed an appeal before the Delhi Sessions Judge, pleading that Nagarwala's conviction be set aside as he had been made to confess under duress. Maheshwari contended that Nagarwala was being subjected to continuous interrogation and was also being tortured in prison. Maheshwari alleged that Nagarwala's confession was influenced by the police, including ASP Kashyap, who had promised that Nagarwala would be rewarded and set free if he confessed to his crime. Nagarwala had believed the police. The judge set aside the conviction and directed that the case be moved to the court of the Additional Chief Judicial Magistrate.

On the same day, Nagarwala was granted bail against an amount of twenty-five thousand rupees. However, for reasons best known to him, Nagarwala declined the offer of bail and instead, opted for a cell in the barracks. According to Shastri, Nagarwala felt that his life would be in danger once he stepped out of prison. In fact, it seemed that Nagarwala was worried after his application for a retrial had been granted in the first place.

As the trial proceeded at snail's pace with various disruptions delaying proceedings, another shocking piece of news made headlines. On November 20, Kashyap, who had led the investigation in the Nagarwala case, died in a road accident, less than a month after his wedding. He was thirty-one years old. In July, Kashyap had been promoted to the rank of Additional Superintendent of Police, with the government declaring that Kashyap's promotion was par for the course and was in no way related to his solving the Nagarwala case in a few hours. Kashyap's death gave rise to several conspiracy theories that were fanned by the media and the Opposition.

***

In January 1972, Nagarwala was hospitalised on several occasions—at Tihar Jail Hospital as well as Irwin Hospital (now, Lok Nayak Jaiprakash Narayan Hospital)—as he kept complaining of chest pain. An ECG performed at Irwin Hospital confirmed that Nagarwala had 'myocardial infarction', a condition where the blood flow to the heart is blocked because of the build-up of plaque in arteries, which deprives the heart of oxygen, causing its muscle cells to die. During his hospitalisation, Nagarwala wrote several letters to his mother, informing her about his condition and also telling her not to worry as the hospital staff were taking good care of him.

When Pudumjee, who was in Bombay, got to know about his friend's hospitalisation, he rushed to Delhi. He met Nagarwala in the hospital and offered to arrange for his bail. However, Nagarwala declined the offer. He believed that if he was in police custody, he would be produced before the magistrate at regular intervals; otherwise, the hearings would be delayed.

On Nagarwala's request, Pudumjee met his lawyer, Maheshwari, and compensated him. The lawyer tried to extract information about Nagarwala's background from Pudumjee, complaining that his client hardly shared any information with him, which was making it difficult for him to fight the case.

Through February, Nagarwala kept shunting between Irwin Hospital and Tihar Jail, as his treatment continued. During one such stay at Irwin Hospital, Pudumjee met him. Unlike previous occasions, Nagarwala appeared keen to be out on bail and fight the case. Pudumjee, who was scheduled to visit Australia for a month to attend a conference, promised that he would arrange for the bail money and get his friend released as soon as he returned to India. When Pudumjee mentioned to Nagarwala that the latter's mother was eager to visit him in Delhi, Nagarwala insisted that she should not be allowed to do so. Being aware that Pudumjee had the right contacts, Nagarwala also requested to be put in touch with eminent personalities from the media, as well as from the movie industry, who would take his story to the world.

Later that month, as Nagarwala's condition deteriorated, he remained under the supervision of several doctors of Irwin Hospital and GB Pant Hospital. On February 22, Goolbai wrote a letter to the Prime Minister, appealing to her maternal instincts and requesting her to intervene. She did not receive any response from the PMO.

At this time, Nagarwala was visited by Om Prakash Malhotra, a retired army official from Ranikhet. Nagarwala had, in the past, helped Om Prakash build a house in Defence Colony in Delhi. Even after Om Prakash had repaid the loan, he continued to send money to Nagarwala, who had, in the meantime, fallen on bad times. It was with the intention of paying the money which he owed to Om Prakash that Nagarwala had planned to visit Ranikhet the day after the robbery.

On March 2, Nagarwala turned fifty. He was visited at GB Pant Hospital by his lawyer, Maheshwari, who handed him flowers and greeting cards from his mother, sister, nephew, and nieces, which made Nagarwala very happy. However, shortly after the lawyer had left, Nagarwala collapsed while eating lunch on his hospital bed. Doctors rushed to his aid and made several attempts to revive him, but all such measures failed, and Nagarwala was declared dead.

The hospital authorities informed Tihar Jail. The jail authorities, in turn, informed Bagli, the manager and priest of the Parsi Dharamshala, who rushed to GB Pant Hospital and offered prayers. Goolbai was devastated on receiving the news. She had been preparing to visit her son the next day. Pudumjee, who was in Melbourne at that time, received the news of his friend's demise on the wire.

Nagarwala's mortal remains were cremated on the night of March 3 in the presence of his mother and friends, after an autopsy had been duly conducted. The autopsy concluded it was a natural death.

With Nagarwala's death, the case was closed, and the money that had been recovered, as well as the car which Malhotra had used to carry the chest loaded with cash, were returned to State Bank of India.

***

In June 1977, after Morarji Desai became the Prime Minister of India, an inquiry commission was set up under Justice Pingle Jaganmohan Reddy to probe specifically into Chief Cashier V. P. Malhotra's withdrawal of sixty lakh rupees from the strongroom of the Parliament Street branch of State Bank of India, the transfer of the money to Nagarwala, the filing of a complaint at the Parliament Street Police Station and the subsequent police investigation, Nagarwala's arrest and the recovery of the stolen money, the possible involvement of an accomplice, Nagarwala's conviction and death during the retrial, and the death of the investigating officer, Kashyap.

Before the Reddy Commission started its inquiries, an article in *India Today* magazine suggested the possibility that Nagarwala was an undercover courier who had been funnelling money to support guerrilla warriors in Bangladesh on behalf of the State, and the government had washed their hands off the matter when it had been reported to the police.

The commission examined nearly two hundred and fifty persons between April and September 1978. Subsequently, in the same year, it issued an 820-page report, wherein it stated that the bank had kept private, unaccounted assets. While there was no direct evidence of the government's involvement in keeping that money in the bank, police investigations into the matter could have been more elaborate without the intervention of certain government officials. The report observed that the confessional statement of Nagarwala should have been rejected, as it was based on only his narration of events and had not been backed by any evidence. Nagarwala's death, however, had been natural, without any hint of foul play.

Over the years, the scandal has continued to fuel debates and rumours, including alleged political motivations, insider collusion, and possible links to covert operations. The case certainly revealed systemic lapses in banking security, particularly the absence of verification processes for high-level requests, prompting reforms. Triggering widespread public and political intrigue, the heist remains a subject of speculation in the history of India's financial crimes.

The Truck Hijackers

Sarvesh cast a cautious glance around as he waited for Pramod to receive the call at the other end of the line. The news he had received a while back was remarkable, and he knew that every second from this moment onwards was crucial. He had to inform Pramod immediately. He had walked to the clearing at the back of the yard of the transport company and placed the call.

The spacious yard of the A to Z Transporting Company was surrounded by boundary walls, with the small administrative office located near the entrance, serving as the hub for dispatch and record-keeping. Much of the yard was dedicated to parking trucks, tempos, and lorries. The yard was abuzz with activity, and vehicles were moving around noisily, leaving clouds of dust in their trail. No one was watching Sarvesh.

Pramod received the call after the third ring. Sarvesh covered his mouth with a hand although there was no fear of being overheard as there was no one in the vicinity. He lowered his voice almost to a whisper and said, 'Pramod *bhai*, I have news for you!'

Pramod was all ears.

It had been a year since Pramod had left his job as a driver at the A to Z Transporting Company in Ghaziabad, Uttar Pradesh. Since then, the going had not been particularly easy for the twenty-five-year-old. There were mouths to feed at home, and he hadn't had enough money over the past year. He had left the job with plans of starting his own transport company. He had contacts in the right places and knew that securing transportation contracts would not be a problem. But he needed seed money to start his business. He was not willing to wait forever to earn that money. There *had* to be an easy way out.

This was where Sarvesh came in. Sarvesh had been his co-worker at the A to Z Transporting Company and still drove canters for them. Sarvesh, too, had dreams of buying his own canter and starting a business of his own. Sarvesh and Pramod had since long bonded over their dreams.

Pramod had asked Sarvesh to let him know if the transport company was going to pick up a large consignment anytime soon. Having driven those canters for many years, Pramod had a fair idea of how one could take a driver down on an empty road and seize the cargo. The two of them were confident that they needed only one chance to change their fate. The consignment, however, had to be large enough to justify the risk involved. Pramod had the contacts and the means of taking care of the rest. Sarvesh had informed him of some large consignments on a few occasions in the past, but they had not piqued Pramod's interest.

Today, Pramod could gauge the purpose of Sarvesh's untimely call.

'Tell me about it,' Pramod said, going straight to the point.

Sarvesh cast a surreptitious glance around once again and said, 'More than twenty-five crores, *Bhai*. Brand new Samsung mobile phones. They will be launched in the market shortly.'

There was a glint in Pramod's eyes as his heart leapt. This was just what he had been dying to hear!

'When?' Pramod asked.

'The night of March 31, *Bhai*,' said Sarvesh.

'Wait for my call,' Pramod instructed before ending the call.

Sarvesh looked at the vast expanse of the field before him. Another warm day was coming to an end. The sky was painted in hues of red and purple, on which homebound birds made strange patterns. The young man of twenty-seven felt that a new chapter of his life was about to begin. He had complete faith in Pramod's scheming, cunning ways.

Pramod, on the other hand, got busy as soon as he ended the call. While he had a broad outline of the plan in mind, he knew that it would not be possible for just the two of them to pull off a heist. Also, considering the nature of the goods—brand new mobile phones that were yet to be launched in the market—he had to arrange for the transportation and disposal of the loot. He would have to enlist the help of some friends, and he knew just who he should reach out to. He had to make a few phone calls.

Over the next few days, Pramod and Sarvesh met on several occasions. They were joined by Pramod's friends—Manku, Neeraj, and Vinesh—as well as Vinod, a twenty-nine-year-old man who worked as a driver at Chauhan Transport in Noida, and his brother, Pramod (Yadav), a twenty-five-year-old man who worked for A to Z Transporting Company.

Before long, the gang had the blueprint for the heist ready, and they waited eagerly for the night that would change their lives forever.

***

Around half past eleven on the night of March 31, 2015, two trucks left from Indira Gandhi International Airport. They were loaded with mobile phone components imported from Korea—integrated circuit chips, motherboards, assembly covers, and the like. The parts were meant for high-end mobile phones to be assembled and launched by Samsung in the Indian market shortly. The estimated cost of the parts was around twenty-six crores. The net worth of Samsung's business at stake was to the tune of two hundred crores. This was a game of high stakes.

The parts were to be delivered to Sector 82, Noida Phase-II, in Uttar Pradesh. Sarvesh was in the driver's seat in one of the trucks. The other was driven by Ghanshyam, a twenty-five-year-old man.

Pramod had been waiting near the airport in a white Tata Sumo, which belonged to Vinesh, who was in the driver's seat. The two were accompanied by Neeraj and Manku.

The illuminated control tower, the brightly lit terminal buildings, and the neon signs of luxury hotels, restaurants, cafes, and retail outlets in the vicinity of the airport stood out against the night sky. Despite the late hour, the area was abuzz with taxis, private cars, buses, and airport shuttles ferrying passengers to and from terminals. Trucks and cargo vehicles could also be seen in transit. The lights of police vehicles and cars of security personnel, patrolling the roads around the airport, flashed in the dark.

Sarvesh was to call Pramod as soon as the trucks with the Samsung consignment started from the airport. The process of loading the trucks was taking longer than expected, and Pramod was getting restless, waiting outside the airport.

'What is going on?'

'Have they cancelled the consignment?'

'Why has Sarvesh not called yet?'

Pramod kept asking these questions of no one in particular as he squirmed restlessly in his seat and frequently checked his phone.

After what seemed like ages, Pramod received a call from Sarvesh.

'We are starting, *Bhai*,' said Sarvesh, his voice characteristically low. 'Note down the numbers of the trucks.'

Pramod dictated the numbers as he heard them, and Vinesh made a note of the same.

Before long, they could see the trucks leaving the airport premises. The Tata Sumo started following the truck that was being driven by Ghanshyam.

Pramod called Sarvesh. 'Keep talking to us about the route the two of you are taking,' he barked orders on the phone, turning its speaker on. He turned towards Vinesh and said, 'Now step on the accelerator, will you?'

Vinesh was all too familiar with this mood of Pramod—he was high-strung, irritable, and ready to explode at any moment. Vinesh did not talk back. As Sarvesh kept relaying the details of the route, Vinesh followed his instructions and drove the Sumo through the dense traffic, tailing Ghanashyam's truck.

Ghanshyam, a simple man who hailed from the village of Salarpur, had always been wary of transporting high-value goods. He had been jittery from the moment the goods had been loaded in his truck at the airport and could not wait to reach his destination and deliver them safely. When he reached an empty road near Kalkaji, he noticed that a white car, which had been following him for quite some time, had suddenly picked up speed and was honking continuously. He had heard of trucks being hijacked on these roads and feared the worst.

'This isn't looking good. I must get them off my back,' Ghanshyam said, turning to the helper, Lucky.

Before long, Ghanshyam realised that the white Sumo was trying to overtake his truck. He stepped on the accelerator. The Sumo followed suit. It kept abreast, now trying to intercept his truck, confirming his belief that something was indeed wrong. This was not just a bunch of rich kids, high on alcohol and drugs, out for a late-night drive.

Ghanshyam panicked. Keeping his eyes on the semi-dark road

ahead and his foot firmly on the accelerator, he asked Lucky to call Sarvesh.

'His line is busy,' Lucky reported after he had tried Sarvesh's phone a few times. Ghanshyam himself tried to reach his colleague a few more times without any luck. Sarvesh was on another call.

The Sumo was dangerously close to Ghanshyam's truck now, the two vehicles racing on the road in the pitch-black night, each trying to outrun the other.

'Who is he talking to?' Ghanshyam screamed in despair, being unable to reach Sarvesh. 'He must have found a new girl!'

The Sumo finally caught up with the truck on a deserted stretch near Sarita Vihar Flyover at Kalindi Kunj in South-East Delhi. The driver of the Sumo swerved wildly with a deafening screech and came to a halt laterally across the road.

Ghanshyam could feel his heartbeat going berserk. His foot pressed down hard on the brakes, and he brought the truck to a grinding halt, the impact throwing him, along with Lucky, forward on the dashboard.

To his horror, Ghanshyam saw one of the doors of the Sumo open and two men jump out. He looked around nervously. There was not a soul around, but for a few stray dogs. The streetlights on that part of the road were not functioning, and the entire area was shrouded in darkness. The warm wind had picked up speed and whistled ominously down the empty road.

'Get the driver out of the truck!' Pramod screamed as Manku and Neeraj jumped out of the Sumo and ran towards the truck. The beams of light from the truck's headlights pierced through the darkness, and in them, even though Ghanshyam could not see the faces of the two men clearly, he could easily make out that one of them was brandishing a gun.

'You two, get down from the truck!' Neeraj wielded his gun and screamed at Ghanshyam and Lucky.

It seemed to Ghanshyam that his limbs were made of lead. He was paralysed with fear. He gulped hard and remained in his seat. So did Lucky. The two men were now standing in front of the truck. Neeraj had his gun trained on Ghanshyam.

In no time, the other man, Manku, climbed up the side of the truck and thrust his head into the driver's cabin. Ghanshyam could feel the stench of Manku's breath fanning his face. Manku grabbed him by the collar of his shirt, which was already drenched in sweat. He slapped Ghanshyam hard across the face.

'Are you deaf?' Manku screamed into his ear.

Ghanshyam opened his mouth, but words failed him.

'Get down from the truck!' Manku screamed again. 'Both of you!' He glared at Lucky.

The next moment, a powerful punch landed on Ghanshyam's jaw. He heard the bone crunch, and the searing pain made him feel nauseous. Before Ghanshyam could react, Manku had flipped a knife open, and Ghanshyam could feel the cold steel blade against his throat. Ghanshyam folded his hands, and tears ran down his cheeks. Without trying to resist any further, he stepped out of the truck, followed by

Lucky. The poor boy had already wet his pants. Ghanshyam saw a door of the Sumo open once again.

Pramod stepped out and walked in long strides towards Ghanshyam and Lucky. Ghanshyam stood rooted to the spot, a hand on his broken jaw, his legs shaking. The man was now standing at arm's length from him. A dog barked somewhere far away.

'You don't need these anymore!' Pramod said, as he snatched the mobile phones from both Ghanshyam and Lucky. Lucky tried to protest but was dealt a blow across his face. Ghanshyam squinted at the man. He looked vaguely familiar. Where had he seen him before? Did he work in the transport company?

Pramod pushed the hapless driver and his helper off the road. Ghanshyam lost balance and landed on the ground on his haunches. Lucky ran to his help. Ghanshyam looked on helplessly as Pramod jumped into his truck. Neeraj and Manku started walking back in the direction of the Sumo. Ghanshyam wondered how many of them were inside the car.

As soon as he got into the truck, Pramod turned his attention to the GPS locator, the fancy toy which the transport company had installed in its vehicles some time back. They were meant to provide security to the trucks as their movements could be monitored from the control room, and deviations from the prescribed routes could be acted upon. Pramod was familiar with the workings of the device, and it did not take him long to deactivate it. He smiled to himself and then started the engine.

'Lie low for a while! All of you have done a good job tonight!' Pramod hollered at his friends as Vinesh drove off past the truck with his two companions in the direction from where they had come.

Pramod stepped on the accelerator and drove off.

Just as Pramod had planned, he was soon joined on the empty road by an Eicher canter that was being driven by Vinod, who was accompanied by his brother, Pramod (Yadav). Vinod honked twice to announce his arrival on the scene, and Pramod reciprocated, as planned. The two trucks sped on dark roads that were flanked on both sides by empty fields and were lined with trees that formed dark blotches on the night sky, the wind moaning ominously through their leaves.

When they reached Hathras in Uttar Pradesh, Pramod pulled up by the road. So did the canter that had been following him. Vinod and Pramod (Yadav) jumped out and joined Pramod. The three men hugged each other and lost no time in getting down to business. 'We have to be quick,' Pramod instructed the two brothers, as the three men started loading the mobile phone parts into the empty Eicher canter.

Once the canter had been loaded, Pramod jumped into the driver's seat of the Eicher canter and stepped on the accelerator, leaving by the roadside the truck they had looted earlier. 'That should fool the cops when they start their investigation tomorrow!' said Pramod, as he looked at his partners and winked.

The canter sped towards Pramod's village in Kasganj. He looked contented, the wind in his hair, his nerves beginning to calm down.

He knew he had managed to pull off a heist that he could tell his grandsons about. '*Mobile company waalon ki toh lag gayi!*' Pramod screamed, and the three men broke into boisterous laughter.

***

When Sarvesh reached the spot close to the Sarita Vihar Flyover, he saw that Ghanshyam and Lucky had been abandoned by the side of the road and their truck looted a short while ago.

'We had been trying to reach you on the phone before the robbers attacked our truck,' Lucky complained. Sarvesh patiently listened to the two, who barely managed to narrate the incident through their pain and shock, and then called up the Police Control Room from his mobile phone, just as Pramod had instructed him.

At about half past twelve, the Sarita Vihar Police Station received information over the phone that a container carrying mobile components had been robbed near the flyover.

Before long, a police team under DCP (South-East) Kuldeep Randhawa and SHO (Sarita Vihar), Parminder Singh, reached the spot. Ghanshyam, Lucky, and Sarvesh were waiting for the police. Ghanshyam repeated his narration of the incident, Lucky filling in wherever necessary, before he was taken away for treatment of his injuries, which had been severely aggravated by that time.

Since both Ghanshyam and Sarvesh had mentioned to the police that the trucks of A to Z Transport Company had been fitted with GPS trackers, the police immediately got in touch with the company and requested that the location of the truck, which Ghanshyam had been driving, be tracked. The company responded after a while, informing the police that the GPS tracker had been disabled.

'This looks like the work of professionals who are familiar with the workings of GPS trackers installed in the trucks of A to Z,' said Kuldeep.

'I won't be surprised if this is the doing of one of their drivers,' said Parminder, adding, 'it looks like an inside job!'

Having played the good Samaritan so that there was no possibility of being considered a suspect, it was time now for Sarvesh to leave. That was the plan he had agreed upon with Pramod. He looked at his watch and feigned concern. He told the policemen, 'I should be leaving now. I should have delivered the consignment long back.'

When the policemen did not heed his pleas, he repeated his request a few times. A few times too many, as it turned out.

'You don't need to worry about the delay in delivery. We will get in touch with the company and let them know,' said Parminder. After a brief pause, he said, 'Ghanshyam said that he had tried to reach you on the phone repeatedly when he had seen the white Sumo tailing his truck, but you had been busy on other calls. Who had you been talking to?' Parminder looked Sarvesh in the eyes and said, 'Let me have a look at your phone.'

Sarvesh could feel his heart skip a beat. This was not part of the script. He was always meant to drive away in his truck after providing whatever information the police were meant to be fed.

His hands visibly shaking, Sarvesh took out his mobile phone from the pocket of his trousers and handed it over to Parminder. There were beads of sweat on his temples, and he licked his dry lips. His anxiety did not escape the eyes of the shrewd cop. Parminder started scrolling through the list of calls in Sarvesh's phone, and his eyes immediately went to a number that Sarvesh had been calling for a surprisingly long duration till some time back.

'Whose number is this?' Parminder asked Sarvesh, whose face had turned ashen in panic and who was sweating profusely, as was evident from the dark, wet patches on his shirt. When Sarvesh tried to answer, his lips moved, but no words escaped his parched lips.

'You are not going anywhere,' Parminder said, gesturing at two of his constables to take Sarvesh to the police station for interrogation. He also ordered that the call data of Sarvesh's phone should be analysed, and the location of the number he had been calling should be traced.

Parminder and Kuldeep formed teams that spread out in different directions, looking for the stolen truck and conducting raids in different parts of Uttar Pradesh. Acting on the possibility that the heist was an inside job and had been engineered by a former employee of A to Z Transport Company, the police started questioning the employees of the company and checking their antecedents and whereabouts on the night of the heist. The police also rummaged through the files at the offices of the company and started checking on employees who had left their jobs in the recent past.

The reports on the call data and tower locations of the mobile phone, which belonged to the person Sarvesh had been talking to, came in. Kuldeep and Parminder learnt that the person had been present at the crime scene and had also been travelling along the same route from the airport, which the trucks had taken!

'Sarvesh had been in touch with this number as Ghanshyam and he had been driving their trucks from the airport. It is evident from the location details of this number that his friend had also been following the same route, and it is likely that he was the one who stole Ghanshyam's truck after leaving him injured near the flyover,' Parminder concluded easily.

'It is interesting that this is the same number with which Sarvesh had been in touch while delivering high-value goods on a few other occasions as well,' said Kuldeep. 'I am sure this is our man!'

The number, it turned out, belonged to Pramod, who had worked earlier for the transport company and had left the job about a year ago. A former employee of the transport company was the mastermind behind Delhi's biggest heist till date, just as the police had suspected.

With irrefutable evidence staring him in the face, it did not take long for Sarvesh to break. He confessed that he, indeed, was the man who had tipped Pramod off. He also gave up the names of all his accomplices.

The police lost no time. Surveillance was beefed up, and teams were mobilised to hunt down Pramod. Before long, Pramod landed up on the radar. The police now knew where he was hiding in the Kasganj district. His movements also came under the hawk eyes of the force.

'We need to act fast before Pramod decamps with the loot,' Kuldeep told his team, as they planned a mission to Kasganj the very next morning.

On the morning of April 2, the police swooped down on Pramod's village.

The village was quiet, with a faint mist lingering over the fields and the first light of dawn breaking through. Most villagers were either asleep or beginning their day with routine tasks like tending to livestock or preparing for the fields. A convoy of police jeeps and vans entered the village, the sound of engines and the glare of headlights shattering the early morning calm.

Armed personnel stepped out of the police vehicles. Officers positioned themselves strategically at the key entry and exit points of the village. Communication was set up through walkie-talkies, ensuring coordinated action. The police knew that the terrain and layout of the village would pose challenges. Narrow lanes and densely packed houses would make navigation and searches challenging. They also knew from experience that strong familial and community bonds often resulted in collective resistance or refusal to cooperate in situations like this.

Kuldeep used a megaphone to call out the names of Pramod, Vinod, and Pramod (Yadav). He issued warnings, urging them to surrender. When a couple of village elders approached him demanding an explanation, Kuldeep apprised them of the purpose of the police mission.

In the meantime, the police had split up into teams to conduct house-to-house searches. Startled villagers, especially women and children, had stepped out of their houses, whispering and watching from a distance.

One of the police teams caught hold of Pramod just as he had been getting ready to leave the village with the loot along with his friends, Vinod and Pramod (Yadav), in the Eicher canter, still loaded with the stolen goods. Realising that escape was impossible, Pramod and his friends surrendered without a fight. The police regrouped and left the village with the detained criminals and confiscated items.

The police vehicles sped off, followed by the Eicher canter loaded with the mobile phone parts, leaving behind a trail of dust.

***

In an interesting turn of events, a few years later, in 2020, Noida police arrested four men who had been stealing display screens, chargers and other mobile phone parts worth eighty lakh rupees from Samsung's warehouse in Noida over several months and sending them to Hong Kong. The police recovered more than twenty lakh rupees from the accused.

The Khalistan Connection

February 12, 1987

It was another busy day at the Millar Ganj branch of the Punjab National Bank, with a mix of customers—businessmen, factory owners, and local residents. Located about sixty miles to the northwest of Chandigarh, the bank experienced heavy footfall as there were several commercial areas in the vicinity.

The town, being close to Ludhiana's industrial zone, was bustling with early-morning activities, with factory labourers and business owners heading to work. The streets near the bank were lined with vendors selling tea, snacks, and other essentials to workers and passersby. Buses, rickshaws, scooters, and cycles jostled for space on the roads. The mid-February morning air was crisp and cold.

A little after nine in the morning, two Matador vans and a Fiat car came to a halt in front of the bank. After around ten minutes, six men in police uniform alighted from the cars and walked into the bank. They carried rifles and submachine guns. One of the two security guards posted outside the bank walked up to what he thought was a team of policemen.

The man leading from the front looked at the guard, even as he gestured at his companions to walk inside. 'There is no reason to panic. We are here to inspect the security arrangements in the bank,' he said in a voice that was firm and reassuring.

The guard immediately stood at attention and saluted the policeman, who summoned one of his companions and asked him to take possession of the guns that the guards were carrying. 'Carry out a thorough inspection of these weapons,' he ordered. The guards duly handed over their guns.

As the leader of the team walked inside, a few members of the staff, including the manager of the branch, left their seats and walked up to him. The manager and his colleagues shook hands with the officer, who exuded unquestionable authority. 'I want complete cooperation from your staff and your customers,' the officer told the manager. 'We will be joined shortly by a few more of our colleagues.'

By a quarter to ten, the bank was teeming with men in uniform—at least twelve to fifteen of them.

The manager pulled a handkerchief out of his pocket and wiped the sweat off his forehead. The unexpected visit by the police to inspect security arrangements in the bank had taken him by surprise.

He started showing the policemen around, explaining the security measures in the bank, finally arriving at a chest, which was located to the left of the entrance to the bank.

This was the moment that the man in charge of the mission had been waiting for. He turned around and smiled at the manager. To his horror, the manager saw that the policeman now had a gun trained on him. 'Thanks for all your help,' the policeman spoke in a calm voice that sent a shiver down the manager's spine. 'I don't want this to be messy. So, please continue to cooperate with my men.'

The manager had not realised that the man in front of him was none other than Sukhdev Singh Dhillon, best known as General Labh Singh, the commander of the Khalistan Commando Force or KCF.

The gradual transformation of a dutiful son, husband, father, and police officer to the man who had masterminded the ingenious plan of robbing a bank was no less fascinating than the wildest imagination of a fiction writer's mind.

***

Sukhdev was born in 1952 in the village of Naushehra Pannuan in Tarn Taran. His father, Puran Singh, was a truck driver. Puran Singh passed away when Sukhdev was young. Sukhdev lived with his mother, Kulwant Kaur, and his brother, Daljit Singh, who was four years older. Of all the family members and friends in Sukhdev's life, he was closest to his cousin, Paramjit. The two of them were inseparable.

Sukhdev studied in Panjwar until the tenth grade and then continued his schooling in a nearby town. Upon graduation, he joined

Punjab Police. On February 14, 1979, Sukhdev married Devinder Kaur. Their first son, Rajeshwar, was born on June 22, 1980.

However, shortly thereafter, Devinder noticed a gradual but steady change in Sukhdev's behaviour. She did not realise when dark clouds had started looming over her happy family. Sukhdev started returning home late from work and offered evasive, often curt, responses when the family enquired about his whereabouts. Most of the time, Sukhdev would say that he was at the Darbar Sahib—a complex in Amritsar that houses the Golden Temple and the Akal Takht, the supreme seat of the Sikh political authority.

The family lamented its growing distance from Sukhdev. He would sit for hours inside a room and meditate, even as his elder son, Rajeshwar, pounded on his door, screaming for his father's attention. There was no significant change in Sukhdev's behaviour, even as Devinder and he welcomed their second son, Pardeep, into the world on November 21, 1982.

Devinder had assumed that the arrival of their second child would help strengthen Sukhdev's bond with the family. However, this was not to be. It had only been three years into their marriage, and yet, Sukhdev had begun to spend very little time with his family. When Devinder questioned her husband, Sukhdev finally declared that he had been visiting *Sant-ji*. Devinder had no idea either about the identity of *Sant-ji* or the reason why he had such a strong impact on her husband.

When Sukhdev was informed that he was going to be posted at Bathinda, a town about a hundred and fifteen miles south of

Amritsar, he declined. Instead, following the Sikh tradition, he took *Amrit,* a holy liquid made from sugar and water, in a ceremony that had been introduced by Guru Gobind Singh and became a Khalsa Sikh, embracing the Sikh Code of Conduct. He transferred the family's belongings to Panjwar and left Devinder and his children at Devinder's paternal house in Tanda Urmar.

The family had no clue about Sukhdev's movements thereafter. Sukhdev was gone for days, and Devinder began to get worried. Finally, one evening, Sukhdev visited his wife. He looked tense and distraught.

'I do not have a lot of time,' he told his wife, 'but I need to tell you something.'

'What is it?' Devinder looked confused and scared.

'The police are after me,' Sukhdev explained to Devinder. 'It's for your own safety and the safety of our children that you should stay away from me for some time.'

'But why are the police after you?' asked Devinder's father. 'What have you done?'

'It's nothing,' Sukhdev said. 'You don't need to worry.'

Having thus warned his family, Sukhdev disappeared into the night.

As Devinder looked at the receding figure of her husband, she wondered how a loyal member of Punjab Police, a lively young man popular among his friends and family, had suddenly become a man on the run. She realised Sukhdev's present circumstances had to do with his association with the *Sant* he had mentioned earlier. Devinder still had no idea who the said *Sant* was. What she also did not know was that her husband was not the only one whose life had taken a dangerous turn. He was but one among the large number of men who had started gathering around the *Sant* at the Darbar Sahib.

The state of Punjab would never be the same again.

***

For the next six months, the family did not hear from Sukhdev. Instead, there were stories coming in from different corners about men having gone missing from their villages for days, leaving families completely in the dark about their whereabouts until one day, they turned up dead in canals or by the river.

Devinder was worried sick about her husband. She spent her days and nights in fear that sat heavy on her chest and almost choked her, counting the hours, waiting for someone to barge into the house with news of Sukhdev having been found dead somewhere. When she could not bear the torture any more, she decided to go out and look for her husband.

Devinder left the village along with her father and her sons and headed towards Amritsar, where she believed she would find Sukhdev. The family arrived at a hostel, Nanak Niwas, that was close to the Darbar Sahib complex. When they wanted to enter, heavily armed guards stopped them.

Devinder was shocked. She had visited the Darbar Sahib earlier, and it had been an open complex with no restrictions on the movements of visitors. As she looked around, she saw men walking around, carrying weapons. There were too many of them! What had changed in the Darbar Sahib suddenly? More importantly, what was her husband doing in a place like this? He was probably still on the run and had taken refuge amidst all these men, who seemed to have effectively shielded themselves from any external influence or authority.

Devinder tried hard to get a grip on her emotions and pleaded with the guards, 'Please allow me inside. I must meet my husband. He used to be in Punjab Police and must have been staying here with *Sant-ji* for last several months. My father is old, and my sons are young. We have travelled all the way from Tanda Urmar for just a glimpse of my husband.'

The guards nodded silently and went away. Devinder hoped that her pleas had not fallen on deaf ears.

After a while, Sukhdev appeared. He no longer wore the beige uniform of the police, which Devinder had got accustomed to seeing on him during the early years of their marriage. He was now in a flowing *chola*.

Devinder was delighted to see her husband alive. In a split second, all her apprehensions and fears, which had kept her up for nights, vanished. She tried to speak, but words failed her. Tears of joy streamed down her cheeks. It no longer mattered that her husband was hiding from the law among heavily armed strangers and that their union was destined to be short-lived. All that mattered was that the father of her children was still alive.

Sukhdev was surprised to see how much his sons had grown during the six months when he had been away from them. He sat down on his haunches and hugged both of them. He then stood up and told Devinder, 'Come with me. I will introduce you to someone special.'

Devinder followed Sukhdev into a room, where security arrangements were tighter than those in the rest of the premises. She saw a tall man sitting cross-legged in the middle of the room. It did not take Devinder long to realise that the man must be the '*Sant-ji*' that her husband had mentioned to her. However, she had expected *Sant-ji* to be someone much older than the man who was sitting in front of her. The man had an aura of composed authority about him, and there were hordes of visitors who flocked into and out of the room in groups to meet him.

The man welcomed Sukhdev's family with a smile. As Pardeep sat on his lap, he looked at Devinder and said, 'Your husband is a good man. Don't worry about him, and don't forget the sacrifices that Sikh women before you have made.'

Devinder nodded, her eyes brimming with tears, though she could not make sense of the *Sant*'s words. All that she understood was that she would never get back the beautiful days of her life, days that now seemed like a distant dream.

The *Sant* was none other than Jarnail Singh Bhindranwale. Bhindranwale and his men believed that the Darbar Sahib needed protection, and they had taken upon themselves the duties of soldiers responsible for its protection. Under the leadership of Bhindranwale, Sukhdev's exploits spread across the length and breadth of the state.

In Sukhdev, Bhindranwale found his brother and named him Labh.

Sukhdev had a new identity as Labh Singh, and before long, he rose through the ranks in Bhindranwale's army through a series of acts of militancy, bank robberies, and assassinations—attempted as well as successful. Stories of the exploits of Labh Singh and his friends spread far and wide, also reaching his family. The *Dhadhi*-s sang paeans about Labh Singh, just like the lore of Robin Hood.

When Punjab Police interrogated Labh Singh's family in Panjwar, they claimed that Labh had fought with the family, run away, and got married. They claimed that they were unaware of where he was or who he had married. In Tanda Urmar, the villagers were told that Devinder's husband was being transferred by Punjab Police from one station to another. Once he had settled down, he would come down to the village and take his wife and children back with him.

In the meantime, when Manbir Singh Chaheru, the first leader of the Khalistan Commando Force, was arrested in 1986, Labh Singh assumed command.

***

One month before the robbery at the Punjab National Bank branch in Millar Ganj, Devinder was in her paternal house when Paramjit, the cousin dearest to her husband, arrived unannounced. He appeared to be in great haste, with no time to lose.

'I have instructions from your husband,' he said to Devinder. 'Pack whatever little you need, pick up your sons and your father, and take a bus to Ludhiana. You should get off at the bypass, and our men will meet you there. You will be taken to a safe house. You will need to stay there for some time.'

Devinder realised that Sukhdev had planned something grand. She did not question Paramjit and did as she had been told.

***

A few days later, as Devinder anxiously waited for her husband in a safe house at the outskirts of Ludhiana, a rickshaw pulled up outside. Two men got off the rickshaw and approached the house, walking through the thick early morning mist that hung over the fields. The tall, thin, turbaned man who walked ahead in brisk steps was her husband, whom everyone now called General Labh Singh.

Devinder was not new to this arrangement. About a year back, General Labh Singh was on trial, accused of killing Ramesh Chander, who was the editor of the *Hind Samachar* newspaper group. Chander was a strong critic of Bhindranwale and had written that Punjab had "become a slaughterhouse". The editor was killed at a busy intersection in Jalandhar. However, the Khalistan Commando Force, under the then militant leader, Manbir Singh Chaheru, in a daring attack on the court premises, opened fire, sprayed bullets for fifteen minutes and freed Labh Singh and three other members of the Khalistan Commando Force from police custody. Ever since the audacious escape, the police kept hunting for the General, and he could meet his wife only on a few occasions in safe houses across Punjab, under the watchful eyes of his army on motorcycles.

'Meet Vicky,' Labh Singh introduced his companion to his wife. The charismatic young man in sunglasses, looking much younger than the General, waved at her. The man's real name was Harjinder Singh Jinda, and in the years to come, he would go on to assume his own place of prominence in the history of Punjab, immortalised by the songs of the wandering *Dhadhi*-s.

After pleasantries had been exchanged, the group boarded the rickshaw again, which headed towards Ludhiana. There, they stayed in a two-storey house in Ghumar Mandi.

Devinder found the residents of the house to be rather interesting.

On the first floor, there was a family that ran a food cart. On the floor above lived a woman named Kamaljit Kaur and her husband, Satnam Singh Bawa, who had taken on the name of Surjit Singh Bijlee. He was the one who had rented the house, introducing himself as an employee in the local electricity board. Kamaljit was a city-bred girl from Ludhiana, who had severed ties with her family after joining the movement. The house also had several visitors, pretty much round the clock. Those were mostly men in the most-wanted list of Punjab Police. The residents were a boisterous lot. The neighbours thought that the occupants of the house belonged to a trucking union, and hence, the perpetual noise and commotion.

While her father and elder son left Ludhiana a couple of days after their arrival, Devinder stayed in the Ludhiana house with her younger son for twenty-one days, enjoying her time there, especially in the company of Kamaljit, Jinda, and of course, her husband.

Little did she know that Labh Singh and his gang had been working on a plan to rob the Punjab National Bank branch in Millar Ganj.

Labh Singh needed money and a lot of it. He had to procure advanced arms and ammunition to continue the militant activities of the Khalistan Commando Force. He needed to forge alliances to support his activities. There was a long list of assassinations that had to be carried out against what the General and his soldiers considered 'state- sponsored terror'.

The branch of the Punjab National Bank at Ludhiana, which Labh Singh had targeted, offered a fantastic opportunity. It had a huge cash reserve, not only because of its proximity to several commercial areas but also because of the funds it held from the Reserve Bank of India. He called upon his most trusted soldiers and built a team for the job. Some of the most prominent members of the Khalistan Commando Force who joined the gang were Harjinder Singh Jinda, Manjit Singh Manju, Paramjit Singh Panjwar, Satnam Singh Bawa, Daljit Singh Bittu, and Gursharan Singh Gama.

On February 12, 1987, these men arrived at the bank, dressed as policemen, supposedly to inspect the security arrangements.

***

As Labh Singh held the manager at gunpoint, his men spread out across the bank. They brandished their guns and ordered customers and members of the staff to squat on the floor.

Labh Singh stretched his hand out before the manager and said in his characteristically calm manner, 'Keys!'

The manager handed him the key to the chest. The cashier had another.

In the next few minutes, Labh Singh and his men opened the chest. They picked up currency notes and valuables worth approximately six crores in Indian Rupees. They took mainly the older soiled notes and did not touch new currency notes. The manager, in his statement to the police, later said that the new currency notes in the chest were worth nearly an additional ten crores. As Labh Singh had found out earlier, part of the money belonged to the Reserve Bank of India, which did not have a branch in the city.

Once the currency notes and valuables had been packed, Labh Singh gestured at one of his men and said, 'Get all the customers and bank officials inside the strongroom and lock them up.'

The customers and members of the staff, who had so far been squatting on the floor, stood up on rubbery legs and were led inside the strongroom. None of them dared to resist.

'There will be no bloodshed as long as each one of you cooperates with us. All we want is to collect funds for the welfare of the *Qaum*,' Labh Singh addressed the men and women packed like sardines inside the strongroom, as he locked the room and put the keys in his pocket. His men standing behind him shouted slogans in support of Khalistan, which reverberated within the walls of the bank.

The men then started distributing the money among themselves. They had been carrying quilt covers, blankets, sacks, and briefcases into which the money and valuables were loaded.

Having completed the operation, the gang left the building and headed towards the vehicles they had parked outside.

As Labh Singh was about to leave the bank, an old man approached him and said, 'Son, I came to the bank to withdraw money. I need only two hundred rupees for a family occasion. The family will be in trouble if I return empty-handed. I would forever be grateful to you if you would be so kind as to give me my money.'

Labh Singh looked at the man who stood in front of him, with his hands folded, his eyes filled with tears.

He untied the blanket that he was carrying. 'Two hundred rupees is quite a small amount for a family function,' he told the old man. 'You may take as much money as you need to make everyone at home happy. As I said, this money is for our *Qaum*.'

The old man embraced the General, overwhelmed with emotion and unable to speak.

The largest bank robbery in the history of the nation at the time was carried out without a single casualty.

News of the robbery spread across the state like wildfire.

Later in the day, a neighbour rushed to Devinder's house in Tanda Urmar and addressed her father, 'Charan Singh, your son-in-law has shaken the state of Punjab today!'

The old man and his daughter exchanged glances, both looking confused. He said, 'Why, what has he done now?'

'He has just taken six crore rupees from a bank in Ludhiana!' the neighbour informed him.

Devinder's father kept looking at his neighbour for a while, his mouth gaping. Then suddenly, he burst into laughter.

'The police will again be coming for us anytime now!' he said amidst peals of laughter.

***

The sensational robbery in broad daylight made headlines across the country and abroad. More than ten thousand security personnel were deployed across Punjab to hunt down the perpetrators. Punjab Police, however, knew that considering the political climate in the state and the fact that the robbery had been carried out by Labh Singh and his men, this would not be an easy investigation.

A few days after the robbery, Paramjit Singh, who was General Labh Singh's cousin, reached Tanda Urmar to meet Devinder. He was accompanied by a friend named Bachittar Singh. The security forces came to know of the visit and with the impression that the two had been part of the gang that had committed the robbery in Ludhiana, surrounded the village. The police rushed into Devinder's house and arrested the two.

Paramjit told the police that he had been worried about Devinder's safety in the wake of the manhunt for Labh Singh and had, hence, visited her from Panjwar. He had a strong alibi as he worked in a government bank and had been in his office on the day of the robbery. Eventually, both Paramjit and Bachittar were released.

However, a week later, the police were back in Devinder's house.

Her nightmare had just started.

***

The police entered the house and ordered Devinder's father to get dressed. Devinder, her father, and Pardeep were then taken to a police station. The three were kept in a cell there.

After the bank robbery, the police had raided the Ludhiana house where Labh Singh had stayed before the heist. They had found a set of photographs, in which the police could recognise Pardeep in a group of children. The photographs had been taken by Jinda, who often took the children out during the time the families spent in the Ludhiana house. In another photograph, Devinder and Pardeep were seen together.

'How did your son turn up at the Ludhiana house?' the police asked Devinder.

'I was ordered to go to Ludhiana. I had no choice but to obey. When we reached Ludhiana, we met Labh Singh, and it was he who took us to that house,' Devinder said.

'For how long did you stay in that house?' asked the police.

Devinder said, 'I was made to stay there for around twenty days against my will. I used to cook and take care of other domestic chores. I wasn't happy doing all the work in that house, because those men had ruined my life. While I was there, one of the men took a picture of Pardeep and me. I don't know who he was.'

When the police asked her to identify the men in some of the pictures, she feigned ignorance and referred to the nicknames that the men had used during their stay in the house.

The police interrogation continued for some time. Devinder and her father were also interrogated by the CBI. While the police were primarily concerned with the whereabouts of Labh Singh, the CBI were interested in the money that had been stolen from the bank. The CBI officials tried to find out if the family had had access to the money.

The three prisoners did not have visitors as no one knew of their whereabouts. One day, a police officer took pity on them and left a pen and paper with Devinder, asking her to write her address down. Later that night, the officer's wife delivered the letter to Devinder's village at Tanda. When the residents of Tanda Urmar blocked the streets outside the Tanda Police Station, they were told that the prisoners had been taken away to Ludhiana. The residents started marching towards Ludhiana, but before long, the police stopped them.

On the 20th day of Devinder's imprisonment along with her father and her younger son, Jinda published an open letter in newspapers across the state, threatening the police and demanding the immediate release of the three prisoners.

The family was released and sent back to the village in Tanda without delay.

After a few weeks, Devinder met her husband secretly in Kashmir. Little did she realise then that it would be their last meeting.

***

Devinder usually had two kinds of guests at her residence. The first were General Labh Singh's 'soldiers'. Like their leader, they were tactful and disciplined. They would make their way through the roads leading to Tanda unnoticed. The second were the police. They would first surround the town and then knock on Devinder's door if they had to question her or take her into custody.

On July 12, 1988, the police arrived at Devinder's residence in Tanda Urmar. However, they conducted themselves differently. They neither made any noise, nor was there a battalion in sight. The police escorted a confused Devinder to a jeep and drove off.

The jeep stopped on a road that went past a field on one side and a few petrol pumps on the other. On reaching the destination, Devinder looked outside the jeep. She could see a large crowd that had gathered on the field. She feared the worst, and her heart skipped a few beats.

The police moved the crowd aside and led Devinder across the field. Her legs felt heavy, and she seemed to be walking in a trance. They stopped in front of the lifeless body of General Labh Singh, drenched in blood, sprawled on the field.

There was a bullet wound in Labh Singh's chest, and he had bled profusely. His arms had also been wounded. His feet and knees were muddy. Some of his nails had partially been removed and were seen dangling. There was a *safa* next to his body, in which his gun and shoes had been packed. As Devinder sat down next to the lifeless body of her husband and ran her fingers through his hair, she was told that the police had seen Labh Singh walking along the field and had ordered him to stop. Labh Singh had disobeyed and started running, and in the resulting encounter, he had been shot dead.

At the time of Labh Singh's death, there was a bounty of one lakh rupees on his head. He was wanted for the murder of at least a dozen policemen and a newspaper editor, as well as the attempted murder of former Director General of Punjab Police, Julio Ribeiro.

Conspiracy theories began to spread like wildfire, especially regarding the money trail after the bank robbery in Ludhiana. Questions were raised about the movements of Labh Singh's accomplices in the days after the Ludhiana robbery and if there had been a betrayal. One thing, however, was certain. The money stolen from the bank in Ludhiana significantly bolstered the resources of the Khalistan Commando Force in days to come.

***

Twenty-five years after the robbery, on the afternoon of November 11, 2012, a specially designated TADA (Terrorist and Disruptive Activities) court sentenced twelve men to ten years of rigorous imprisonment. A few others had already been killed in the intervening years in clashes with Indian security forces.

Those convicted included Daljit Singh Bittu, who was fifty-two years old at the time of conviction and had already served a sentence for more than eleven years as an undertrial, and Gursharan Singh Gama, who had also been in jail as an undertrial for close to ten years. They were later released.

Asa Singh, who was ninety-three years old at the time of conviction, was also released afterward.

The verdict was later challenged in the Supreme Court by nine convicts.

On January 10, 2017, the Supreme Court acquitted all the nine convicts on the grounds that the CBI had not been able to prove that the amount of sixty lakhs of rupees that had been recovered from them was part of the six crores of rupees that had been looted from the Punjab National Bank branch at Millar Ganj, Ludhiana, in 1987.

Today, the robbery is analysed in the context of the turbulent political situation in Punjab during the 1980s, marked by widespread violence, human rights violations, and a breakdown of law and order. It is part of the broader history of the Khalistan movement, which remains a deeply contested and sensitive topic among Sikhs.

Many Sikhs, sympathetic to the Khalistan cause, view the robbery as a symbolic blow against a state they perceived as oppressive toward the Sikh community. The funds were reportedly used to finance the separatist movement, including acquiring weapons, supporting the families of militants, and furthering the cause of Khalistan. In Sikh cultural history, the robbery is often recounted in folk songs and stories. These narratives emphasise the bravery, planning, and commitment of Labh Singh and his associates, framing them as martyrs for the Sikh cause.

On the other hand, moderate Sikhs and other observers criticise the act as a criminal offence that undermined the moral high ground of the movement. They argue that such actions alienated public support and reinforced negative stereotypes about militants.

While opinions on the Punjab National Bank robbery by Labh Singh vary, it remains a significant chapter in the history of Punjab, reflecting the complexities and controversies of the Khalistan movement and the era's political turmoil.

References

1. "1987 Opera House Heist". Wikipedia. https://en.wikipedia.org/wiki/1987_Opera_House_heist
2. "Story of unsolved opera house burglary in Mumbai, Rs 30-L heist amused everyone by its slick execution." https://economictimes.indiatimes.com/story-of-unsolved-opera-house-burglary-in-mumbai-rs-30-l-heist-amused-everyone-by-its-slick-execution/articleshow/18619056.cms
3. "1987 theft, police still in the dark." https://web.archive.org/web/20140323232023/http://archive.mid-day.com/news/2010/may/090510-tribhuvandas-bhimji-zaveri-robbery-1987-police-still-clueless.htm
4. "Conman in CBI garb loots Bombay's leading jewellers Tribhovandas Bhimji Zaveri." https://www.indiatoday.in/magazine/crime-stories/

story/19870415-conman-in-cbi-garb-loots-bombays-leading-jewellers-tribhovandas-bhimji-zaveri-798743-1987-04-14

5. "Mumbai cops still clueless about a 1987 theft." https://www.ndtv.com/cities/mumbai-cops-still-clueless-about-a-1987-theft-417485

6. "Haryana bank robbery worth Rs 100 crore, claim locker owners." https://www.indiatoday.in/india/story/haryana-bank-robbery-pmo-225161-2014-10-30

7. "Dramatic bank heist brings PMO to Sonipat." https://indianexpress.com/article/cities/chandigarh/dramatic-bank-heist-brings-pmo-to-sonipat/

8. "Daring heist in Haryana, thieves dig 125-ft tunnel to loot bank." https://www.deccanherald.com/india/daring-heist-haryana-thieves-dig-2222032

9. "Haryana bank heist: Two suspects arrested." https://www.business-standard.com/article/news-ians/haryana-bank-heist-two-suspects-arrested-114103001016_1.html

10. "Haryana bank heist: Two suspects arrested, building owner's body found." https://www.business-standard.com/article/news-ians/haryana-bank-heist-two-suspects-arrested-building-owner-s-body-found-114103001212_1.html

11. "Sonipat heist plotter found dead as cops crack case." https://timesofindia.indiatimes.com/city/chandigarh/sonipat-heist-plotter-found-dead-as-cops-crack-case/articleshow/44988677.cms

12. "Sonipat bank robbery: Three held, Haryana Police claim 'mastermind' is dead." https://indianexpress.com/article/india/india-others/bank-robbery-3-held-mastermind-dead/

13. "Lure of big-time money led to Gohana robbery." https://www.hindustantimes.com/punjab/lure-of-big-time-money-led-to-gohana-robbery/story-CysHp1mSdFJ4Rk5qtAuwiP.html

14. "Gohana heist: 43 kg jewellery, 2 lakh cash recovered so far." https://www.business-standard.com/article/pti-stories/gohana-heist-43-kg-jewellery-2-lakh-cash-recovered-so-far-114110301142_1.html

15. "Mystery death of Gohana heist 'mastermind' adds new twist." https://www.rediff.com/news/special/mystery-death-of-gohana-heist-mastermind-adds-new-twist/20141103.htm

16. "Gohana's great bank robbery." https://www.tribuneindia.com/news/archive/people/gohana-s-great-bank-robbery-7391/

17. "Gohana bank heist: Key accused held." https://timesofindia.indiatimes.com/city/chandigarh/chandigah/articleshow/45237347.cms

18. "How 4 Men Pulled Off Delhi's Biggest Heist. Almost." https://www.ndtv.com/delhi-news/4-arrested-for-26-crore-robbery-in-delhi-of-truck-loaded-with-samsung-phone-parts-751956

19. "Truck carrying Samsung phone parts hijacked on way to Noida plant." https://indianexpress.com/article/cities/delhi/truck-carrying-samsung-phone-parts-hijacked1/

20. https://newsroom24x7.com/2015/04/04/delhi-police-solves-sensational-robbery-samsung-mobile-phone-parts-worth-rs-26-crore-recovered/

21. "Delhi's 25-Crore Robbery of Truck Loaded With Samsung Phone Parts." https://www.ndtv.com/cities/in-delhis-biggest-armed-robbery-goods-worth-rs-25-crore-gone-751760

22. "Robbers hijack truck with phone parts worth Rs 26 crore, caught." https://timesofindia.indiatimes.com/city/delhi/robbers-hijack-truck-

with-phone-parts-worth-rs-26-crore-caught/articleshow/46789810.cms

23. "Rs 26-cr e-goods heist in Kalindi Kunj." https://www.dailypioneer.com/2015/page1/rs26-cr-e-goods-heist-in-kalindi-kunj.html
24. "Goods worth Rs. 25 crore looted in Delhi's biggest heist." https://www.business-standard.com/article/news-ians/goods-worth-rs-25-crore-looted-in-delhi-s-biggest-heist-115040201056_1.html
25. "Delhi Police Look to Recover Stolen Samsung Electronics Components." https://www.gadgets360.com/mobiles/news/delhi-police-look-to-recover-stolen-samsung-electronics-components-677519
26. "Four held in Delhi Rs. 26 crore goods heist." https://www.business-standard.com/article/news-ians/four-held-in-delhi-rs-26-crore-goods-heist-115040300776_1.html
27. https://www.thehindu.com/news/national/other-states/samsung-phone-parts-worth-80-lakh-stolen-from-warehouse-4-arrested/article32133652.ece
28. "This train heist in Tamil Nadu had the sleuths at their wits' end for months." https://www.thehindu.com/news/cities/chennai/this-train-heist-had-the-sleuths-at-their-wits-end-for-months/article67288528.ece
29. "Salem-Chennai train heist case: Robbers claim they burnt 2 crore in cash after demonetisation." https://www.thehindu.com/news/cities/chennai/train-robbers-claim-they-burnt-2-crore-in-cash/article25465385.ece
30. "Their Train Heist Went Like Clockwork. Demonetisation Left Loot Useless." https://www.ndtv.com/tamil-nadu-news/demonetisation-left-loot-useless-salem-chennai-egmore-express-heist-went-like-clockwork-1946492

31. "After two years, two arrested in Salem train heist case." https://www.newindianexpress.com/nation/2018/Oct/14/after-two-years-two-arrested-in-salem--train-heist-case-1885259.html

32. "The Great Train Robbery: Rs 5.78 crore stolen from consignment of Rs 342 crore on the way to Chennai." https://www.newindianexpress.com/cities/chennai/2016/Aug/09/the-great-train-robbery-cash-stolen-from-consignment-of-rs-342-crore-on-the-way-to-chennai-1507449.html

33. "Chennai: Rs 5.78 crore train heist cracked." https://timesofindia.indiatimes.com/city/chennai/chennai-5-78-crore-train-heist-cracked/articleshow/66201313.cms

34. "CB-CID cracks Salem-Chennai train robbery, arrests two men." https://timesofindia.indiatimes.com/city/chennai/cb-cid-cracks-salem-chennai-train-heist-arrests-two-men/articleshow/66197560.cms

35. "Salem train heist case: Five more held in Madhya Pradesh, brought to Chennai." https://www.newindianexpress.com/states/tamil-nadu/2018/Oct/31/salem-train-heist-case-five-more-held-in-madhya-pradesh-brought-to-chennai-1892368.html#:~:text=On%20August%208%2C%202016%2C%20a,CID%20on%20August%2011%202016.

36. "2016 Salem-Chennai Express heist: two Madhya Pradesh gang members arrested." https://www.thehindu.com/news/cities/chennai/2016-salem-chennai-express-heist-two-madhya-pradesh-gang-members-arrested/article25217155.ece

37. "Salem train heist: DSP-led team gets vital clues in MP." https://www.deccanchronicle.com/nation/current-affairs/141018/salem-train-heist-dsp-led-team-gets-vital-clues-in-mp.html

38. "Chennai: Salem-Chennai train heist: CB-CID arrests 5 more accused." https://www.deccanchronicle.com/nation/current-affairs/311018/chennai-salem-chennai-train-heist-cb-cid-arrests-5-more-accused.html

39. "When Demonetisation Shattered Dreams of Robbers Who Looted Over Rs 5 Crore From Train." https://www.news18.com/news/india/when-demonetisation-shattered-dreams-of-robbers-who-looted-over-rs-5-crore-from-train-1937205.html

40. "The Man Behind The 2016 Train Heist." https://www.magzter.com/stories/Newspaper/The-Hindu/The-Man-Behind-The-2016-Train-Heist

41. "The Nagarwala case: Is the truth buried?" https://www.indiatoday.in/magazine/cover-story/story/19770430-the-nagarwala-case-is-the-truth-buried-823665-2014-08-06

42. "Nagarwala case." Wikipedia. https://en.wikipedia.org/wiki/Nagarwala_case

43. "November 5, 1978, Forty Years Ago: Nagarwala Case." https://indianexpress.com/article/opinion/editorials/november-5-1978-forty-years-ago-nagarwala-case-5433856/

44. Kidwai, Rasheed and Prakash Patra. *The Scam That Shook a Nation: The Nagarwala Scandal*. HarperCollins India.

45. "Labh Singh." Wikipedia. https://en.wikipedia.org/wiki/Labh_Singh

46. "30 years on, bank still bears marks of Rs 5.7 crore robbery." https://timesofindia.indiatimes.com/city/ludhiana/30-years-on-bank-still-bears-marks-of-rs-5-7-crore-robbery/articleshow/56490183.cms

47. "SC acquits 12 in 1987 robbery case." https://indianexpress.com/article/india/sc-acquits-12-in-1987-robbery-case/

48. "Sikh separatists take $ 4.5 million in bank heist." https://www.upi.com/Archives/1987/02/12/Sikh-separatists-take-4.5-million-in-bank-heist/9831540104400/

49. "Sikh Separatists Masquerade as Police to Stage India's Biggest Bank Robbery." https://www.latimes.com/archives/la-xpm-1987-02-13-mn-2178-story.html

50. Singh, Rattanamol. "Labh: A General, His Wife & The 1980s Sikh Insurgency." http://lhouse.co/

51. "5.6 cr heist: Bittu gets 10-yr RI." https://timesofindia.indiatimes.com/city/ludhiana/5-6cr-heist-bittu-gets-10-yr-ri/articleshow/17306485.cms

52. "SC acquits 12 in 1987 robbery case." https://indianexpress.com/article/india/sc-acquits-12-in-1987-robbery-case/

53. "1987 Ludhiana bank heist: SC acquits 9." https://www.tribuneindia.com/news/archive/courts/1987-ludhiana-bank-heist-sc-acquits-9-348815/